For the seekers,
the silent rebels,
and those who choose truth over comfort.

"We are living in a computer-programmed reality, and the only clue we have to it is when some variable is changed, and some alteration in our reality occurs."
— Philip K. Dick, *1977 Metz Sci-Fi Conference*

"The privilege of a lifetime is to become who you truly are."
— Carl Jung

PROLOGUE

"You have died three times already. This is your fourth and final chance to remember."

There was a time when the stars spoke in clear voices.

Before language was owned. Before silence was weaponized.
Before the Veil coiled itself around the minds of the many.

In that time - before time - there were those who walked between.
Scribes of the unseen. Carriers of flame. Rememberers.

They were not kings. Not priests. Not warriors.
They were ordinary ones who remembered the extraordinary.
They did not build temples.
They became them.

But something came.
A shadow not from outside, but from the forgetting within.
And with it: a bargain. Subtle. Perfect.

"You will be safe. You will be fed.
You will no longer ache.
In return…
You will never ask who you are."

Most accepted.

They called it Progress. Stability. Peace.
But it was not peace - it was sedation.
Not stability - but a stillness that suffocates.

And so the dream was lost.
The bloodlines of the rememberers scattered.
Their stories erased.
Their symbols turned to decoration.
Their fire, dimmed…

Until now.

The Sound Beneath the Noise

The alarm blared like a prison siren. Not music. Not birdsong. Just a synthetic scream that Jonah Vale had programmed years ago and never bothered to change.

He reached out from the warmth of sleep like a diver breaking surface, slapped the snooze, and stared at the ceiling. It was cracked in the corner and there was a mould bloom shaped like an eye - he saw it every morning, and it never stopped looking back. Outside, the city murmured its endless liturgy; car horns, air brakes, neon buzz, a far-off argument about nothing.

He swung his legs over the edge of the bed and rubbed the sleep from his eyes like it was guilt. The floor was cold, and the air felt heavy and stale. He padded into the bathroom. Eyes still half closed, he reached instinctively for the ceiling cord for the light. Click. The light buzzed once before flickering into life, washing the room in that slightly too-blue tone that always made him look hungover, even when he wasn't. He exhaled, blinking at his own reflection. Not terrible. Not great. Somewhere in the realm of functionally unremarkable. His hair was a little too unruly, and he had that shadow under his eyes that never quite went away. The first big decision was whether he should bother shaving. He reached for his toothbrush instead; decision made.

"Maybe start sleeping like a normal person," he muttered to himself.

The morning hadn't truly started until his coffee; strong, bitter and instant. The kettle was slow and the fridge hummed too loud. He flipped the lid on his laptop which was on the kitchen table sat amongst a small forest of half-drunk coffee cups. The screen glowed to life. His inbox already had thirty unread emails and he skimmed for anything urgent:

"Mr. Vale, can you make the influencer sound more 'authentic'?"
"Deadline moved up. Client wants edits before lunch."
"Hey Jonah, long time - can you ghostwrite a piece for my crypto-fasting startup?"

He cursed under his breath and turned back to the kettle and opened a cupboard door - no clean cups.

"For fuck's sake." He muttered.

He tried to clean one of the cups from the table, but the scummy ring around the top proved too hard to remove. He filled it anyway and sat down at his computer again. He was good at vanishing into other people's words. Sometimes it scared him how easily he could disappear, and he glanced at a printout of a manuscript next to the computer; one of his own, sat, unfinished for months. His eyes rested on the title for a beat: *The Memory Between Lives*. He thought... *To raw. Too Weird. Too...him*. He put his coffee cup down a little too hastily right on the manuscript and the contents spilled onto the front page, soaking in and bleeding the writing.

Jonah's day job was in content strategy for a wellness startup, or, as he liked to think of it; selling artificial peace through spiritual buzzwords. Today's project was rewriting a product page for their new "mindful microdosing" gum. He opened the file and typed:

"Focus your mind. Free your day. One chew at a time."

"Your calm, conveniently wrapped."

He took a long sip of bitter coffee and then deleted it all. His phone buzzed and his boss's number lit up.

"Sorry Jonah…I know it's early!" she chirped down the phone.

"Hey River. Ok, no worries…I was up and about anyway."

"Great…you get the message about the deadline being brought forward?"

"Sure, yes…I'm on it. I'll send a few thoughts over first, then come into the office. Ok?"

She'd not finished. Jonah leaned back in his chair, phone pressed between shoulder and ear as River's voice rattled on about deadlines. His pen tapped idly at the margin of the notepad in front of him, marking out little scratches and lines while he murmured half-responses.

Without thinking, the pen began to trace something more deliberate: a five-pointed star, lopsided at first, then firmer, with a curved almond-shaped line set neatly inside it. It looked almost like an eye staring back at him from the page. He frowned, a flicker of unease rippling through him before he even understood why.

River was still talking. Jonah gave a distracted grunt of agreement, tore the page free, and crumpled it in his fist. He tossed it toward the kitchen bin, missed, and let it lie on the floor where it landed. He picked his pen back up and turned his attention to the work on the desk, voice flattening again into the practiced tones of someone only half-listening. He snapped back to River who was just wrapping up.

"Great, I know you've still got it *old guy*." The emphasis was to do with the fact that it was his birthday today. She laughed at her own joke, "So make it pop!"

He laughed back, humourless, "Thanks Riv. You know we're heading out a bit later…"

She interrupted, "I heard…sorry dude, hot yoga. Besides, I'm not sure they'll let Gen Z's in." She laughed again. "Come see me when you're in, yes?"

"Definitely..."

Jonah stared at the screen which had timed out. His reflection in the dark monitor looked ten years older than he was, so he hit the space bar and looked at the blinking curser and wrote:

"Suppress the scream - subtly."

His phone pinged.

Mum: "Jonah, wishing you a happy birthday! Call if you get chance."

He didn't reply.

Clarke (ex-colleague): "Bro. 33! Jesus's age. Enlightenment pending...but definitely not tonight 😊 See you later..."

Elliot (coworker): "HB Jonah! Sent something your way. Should get it today."

He smiled wryly; It was probably a book. Or a weird mug. Or one of those mood-lifting incense packs that smell like wet chalk. Elliot had organised drinks for tonight, so he'd find out.

Then another:

Sadie (old flame): "Hey J... wasn't sure if I should text. Hope you're good. Happy Birthday. Stay weird. Sx"

He stared at that last one. "Fuck." He muttered, squirming slightly in his seat. The sex was...wild, but it had ended badly. He wondered why he'd not deleted her number.

He sighed and looked around his apartment; he felt that things hadn't moved on too much since her. No partner. No pets. No plants. Just three potted cacti he

11

named after prophets - Ezekiel and Elijah. The last one he called Cunt, because he couldn't think of any other prophets and that was the first word that came into his head.

He shook it off and decided he'd focus for half an hour. He pushed thoughts of Sadie out of his mind and hunkered over his computer thinking instead about his mindful microdosing gum:

"Chew. Breathe. Forget you were infinite."

"Feel less. Think just enough. Obey better."

After a few cups of coffee, he stretched, sniffed an armpit and winced. He snapped his computer shut and headed for the bathroom. He did a practiced tilt of his head to avoid the light cord which hung inconveniently in the doorway. Like a lot of things in his apartment, he'd never quite got round to changing it. He took another look at himself in the mirror and decided he'd have a birthday shave after all. He opted to do it in the shower and congratulated himself on the micro hack. A few minutes saved.

He stuffed his computer in a bag, and opened his fridge, thinking about lunch. In the door were a pile of protein bars which were freebies from his company; one of the campaigns they'd run. The rest of the fridge was empty. He put a bar in his bag and closed the fridge.

He snatched his lanyard, which hung on the security chain of the front door and swung it over his head. He opened the front door, and there, sat on the floor, was a package. It was wrapped in brown paper, hand-addressed, no logo. He squinted at it, and flipped it over. It felt...old, heavy. He thought...*shit, I hope no one has spent actual money on me.* He felt an uncomfortable obligation rise in him. He shook it off, shrugged and stepped back into the apartment. Then he thought about Elliot's message and smiled to himself, throwing the package onto the dining table amongst all the coffee cups.

He walked into the corridor and double-locked the apartment door behind him. The lift had an old metal concertina door, and Jonah approached somewhat cautiously, pressing the call button. There was a distant click, then an electronic buzz, then...nothing. He looked through the criss-cross door down the shaft. Nothing. He cursed again, shouldered his bag and headed to the stairwell.

Jonah stepped out into the marble-and-concrete lobby, gasping for breath and rubbing his temple.

Graham, the building's porter, was mopping near the front desk - elderly, leathery, and somehow always mid-chuckle even when alone. He was humming an off-key tune that may have once been Sinatra and he looked up at Jonah who was leaning against the wall. As he stood next to the lift, it leapt into life and groaned as it headed upwards.

"I'm impressed with this new exercise routine Jonah." Graham smiled, knowingly.

"Fucking thing...she hates me."

"Poor Bessie, she's just old is all." He nodded towards the lift. "What about you? Still among the living, are we?" Graham paused from his mopping.

Jonah smirked. "Physically, maybe. Mentally? That's still under review."

Graham chuckled, his laugh like gravel in a tin can.

"Didn't hear you come in last night."

"That's because I didn't leave yesterday," Jonah replied, rubbing one eye, his breath recovering. "Slept like a corpse."

"A corpse wouldn't still owe rent."

Jonah let out a dry laugh, heading for the door.

"Cheers for the reminder, Graham. I'll think about paying once you get Bessie doing her job."

"Anytime, lad. Oh - and keep an eye on the pigeons by the bins. Think they're organising." He dipped his mop in the bucket again, and sarcastically. "They're just around that corner by the way, the bins." He winked.

Jonah gave him a wry smile. "I'll let you know if they unionise."

Graham chuckled and went back to mopping, the rhythm of it oddly steady - as if it were the most important task in the building.

As he headed for the exit, Jonah turned.

"You didn't see anyone leave a package last night, did you?"

Graham broke his rhythm again. "Walk all those stairs? No one's that daft. And old Bessie's loud enough to wake a corpse." He winked. "So, no lad. They'd usually leave it with me, unless...you've not been ordering anything that needs batteries, have you?" He twinkled.

Jonah smiled and shook his head. "No worries, just thought I'd ask..."

The Polished Cage

The office was on the fifth floor of a converted warehouse with exposed brick, shared plant cuttings, and the faint, ever-present scent of matcha.

A neon sign on the far wall read: "Realign. Reawaken. Reinvest."

Jonah arrived just after nine, dodging a skateboard parked by the coat rack and stepping over a pile of branded yoga mats.

The workspace was open plan, all glass and echo, peppered with ergonomic furniture and scattered Himalayan salt lamps that no one ever switched on. Jonah headed for the smoothie station and poured himself a coffee. Two interns were comparing fasting windows.

"I've moved to 18:6,' one whispered reverently. 'But I still microdose coffee during the off-hours."

Jonah ignored them and threaded through with his coffee. He dropped his bag beside his desk—an overly minimalist white rectangle nestled between a cactus and a half-dead rubber plant. The plant guarded the entrance to his space, and he'd planted a small sign in the soil that had a red and a green slider. Next to green it said: *Welcome*, next to the red it had said: *Sorry Busy*. He'd crossed that out and sharpied in: *Fuck Off*. The slider was fixed on red, and he'd secured it with a piece of chewed mindfulness gum. He slid into his seat and took a breath. Someone had left a wellness crystal on his keyboard again. It vibrated with vague menace and he picked it up and threw it into the potted plant where a small collection was growing.

"Morning, mate."

He looked up to see Terry from Finance perched on his desk divider, peeling a banana with the bored aggression of someone who'd already skimmed the entire Premier League newsfeed.

"United played like they'd been hypnotised," Terry muttered.

Jonah settled into his seat. "Maybe they just realised they still get paid ten years salary *every week*…even if they just run around the pitch doing nothing." Jonah offered, booting up his computer.

Terry scoffed, banana mid-bite.

"You've got no soul, mate. That's the problem. You lot think football's about money. It's *religion*. It's the last real thing we've got left - ninety minutes where the world makes sense."

He gestured dramatically with the banana, like a prophet with a soggy scroll.

"You ever felt forty thousand people hold their breath at the same time? That's church, Jonah. *Church.*"

Jonah raised an eyebrow as he sipped his coffee.

"Church? Funny, I always thought church involved fewer beers, more guilt, and less shouting at the VAR."

Terry shook his head in mock disgust.

"Blasphemy. You'll never be saved, mate."

"Already damned, Terry. I work in digital wellness marketing."

Terry realised he wasn't getting any more and disappeared behind the divider once again. As his desktop hummed to life, Jonah opened Slack and pinged Elliot.

"Hey mate, thanks for the gift. Pretty sure it arrived already. Mysterious brown package on the doorstep?"

Elliot wrote back within seconds; "Huh? Nah mate - I sent it to the office. Should be coming later today. Unless Amazon's astral projectin' now."

Jonah paused, frowning. "Right... must've been something else then."

He stared at the screen a second longer and something flickered in the corner. A shape - circular, spiralled, like a symbol - but it blinked away too fast to catch.

He blinked. The desktop was normal, the cursor flashing, waiting.

His phone buzzed on his desk. River was chasing him up.

"Jonah," his boss chimed through the headset. He took the hint…

"Yep, on my way…"

Her office was a glass fishbowl, looking out onto the open plan floor. He didn't enter fully but stood in the door and leant against the frame. She looked up from behind three monitors.

"Jo Jo…can you make the new copy less... cosmic? People like the *idea* of expansion, but not the responsibility of it." She snorted. "All feels a bit…you know…heavy!"

Jonah looked at her blankly. "Cosmic. Right. Light on the soul evolution, heavy on the subscription model."

"Exactly." She lit up, then paused. "And make sure we say organic four times. It tests well."

"Got it."

He turned and left before she could say anything else. He sat heavily at his desk and rubbed both hands on his face then reached for his coffee. It had gone cold and he grimaced, pouring the remains into the rubber plant. He got up to get a top up and saw the interns were running a mini-sound bath in the kitchenette, so he cursed and sat down again. He reached for the protein bar in his bag.

The hum of the office was the same as always - a quiet storm of keystrokes, muffled coughs, and the occasional muted chuckle from a colleague's headphones. The overhead lighting buzzed faintly in its usual fluorescent migraine. Jonah sat at his desk and felt it once again. There was a deep ache, a sense that there was something important that he'd forgotten but couldn't quite grasp what it was.

It was always there beneath the surface.
A whisper under the hum of the fridge.
A rhythm in the train tracks.
A message in the static:

"You were not born for this."

He'd always tried to do the right thing.

University. Degree. Job in the city. He ticked the boxes with quiet diligence, like someone following a sacred map etched by other people's expectations. He wore a suit that never quite belonged to him and worked in a tower of glass where he repackaged illusions and sold them at a premium. Financial products, bundled like lies in origami - folded and refolded until no one could tell what they really were. He moved numbers from one ledger to another, took a fee, and called it creation.

Every morning, he walked beneath six-foot-high value statements etched in brushed chrome on the walls of the bank lobby - Integrity. Innovation. Impact. But Jonah knew that the only impact was on the balance sheets of people already drowning in excess. The pool he swam in was shallow, and even then, it never touched the skin of anything real.

Still, he stayed, and his friends did the same. They all laughed over craft beers and compared bonus structures; they clicked glasses and wore smiles like masks. He bought an apartment, leased a car, added a motorbike to the garage just to feel something sharp in his lungs on Sunday mornings. And he wrote - late at night, in the quiet, when the ache in his gut made it impossible to sleep. Words were the only thing that touched the edges of the emptiness. They circled it. Named it. Carved some meaning out of the fog.

His therapist called it abandonment trauma. Said it traced back to the moment his father left - slamming the door so hard the world seemed to tilt, never to be seen again. His mother raised him with a spine of iron and a tongue dipped in bitterness. She had no softness left to give and Jonah became her reluctant altar of resentment. He learned early how to make himself small, how to be good. How to be needed, instead of known.

He quit the bank the day he realised the ache wasn't going anywhere. It didn't matter how well he performed or how much money he made - his soul wasn't interested in metrics.

The startup felt like a lifeboat: something fresh, something noble, something good. Health products, mindfulness, wellness: words that hinted at healing. He took a pay cut and told himself it was a sacrifice for something better. Maybe now he could write more, create, connect to something that felt real. At least the kombucha was free, and the lunch options weren't bad.

But within months, he saw the same architecture - new paint, same bones. Different slogans, same exploitation. The metrics were different, but the game was the same: chase dopamine, polish optics, sell hope in recyclable packaging.

Instead of soothing the ache, the job fed it, and now it came with an aftertaste of betrayal. Not of the world - but of himself.

Maybe it wasn't the job. Maybe it wasn't the system. Maybe it was *him*.

Maybe he *was* the wrong shape for this world.

And if not here… where?

He asked the question daily, like a prayer with no recipient. And as the answer continued its silent retreat, so did his life. The apartment, gone. The car, gone. The careful scaffolding he'd built to hold up a self he didn't recognise - it collapsed, piece by piece, as if returning him to the raw material of who he really was.

It was in that rubble, perhaps, that the remembering would begin. Perhaps.

A feeling started to well up, like an acrid indigestion and he felt as though he may throw up.

Then his screen glitched again. A series of symbols filled his screen then disappeared. He rubbed his eyes and picked the protein bar wrapper out of the bin to see if there was anything in it that may have caused indigestion. As he squinted at the wrapper, Elliot slid into the space beside him.

"Birthday boy," he grinned. "We're hitting that weird bar you pretend not to like. You in?"

Sarah from design perked up behind her monitor.

"Wait - it's *your* birthday? No way. What star sign is that?"

"The existentially disappointed one," Jonah muttered.

"So Capricorn," Elliot whispered.

They all laughed.

"We'll meet at that basement place after eight," Elliot said. "Be there…it's your show dude."

Jonah nodded. "Yeah, I'll be there. Just need to finish this last bit."

As the others filtered out, River appeared at his desk, coat slung over one shoulder, her boots clicking a rhythm of rushed authority.

"Jonah - sorry. I meant to say earlier. Can you tweak that affiliate pitch deck before morning?"

He looked at her for a beat, his eyes flitted to the time on his monitor. "Sure. I'll send it before I leave."

"You're the best." She offered a tight smile. "And happy birthday, by the way. Go easy on the existential dread, yeah?" She looked at the sign in his rubber plant then vanished out the door, leaving the scent of patchouli and pressure in her wake.

The office fell silent, and Jonah opened the pitch deck.

As he began typing, the screen glitched again. Just for a second.

The interface stuttered, pixelated, then flashed a string of symbols - like ancient runes - before snapping back to normal.

He blinked.

His skin prickled.
He minimized the window.
Looked around the room like someone was watching.

He was midway through rewriting the pitch deck's call-to-action when the building's buzzer echoed through the quiet office.

He blinked at the sound. Checked the time - 6:27 p.m.

A moment later, the delivery guy appeared at the glass doors, holding a small cardboard box with a bright orange sticker: "Prime - Chill Vibes Inside."

Jonah signed for it, vaguely puzzled, and returned to his desk.

He opened it. It was from Elliot.

Inside was a palm-sized plastic banana Buddha, complete with tiny round sunglasses and a belly full of unknowable joy. It bobbed left to right as the light caught the solar strip.

A yellow Post-it fluttered out.

"Thought you could use something truly enlightened on that bleak desk of yours. May his potassium levels bring you inner peace. - E."

Jonah stared at the thing.

It grinned back at him.

He smiled - actually smiled - but it didn't quite reach his eyes. The juxtaposition between the dancing banana and the strange, spiralled symbols from earlier felt like cosmic satire.

"Thanks, Elliot," he muttered. "Right on schedule."

He placed it on the desk and it wobbled back and forth.

The Birthday Gathering

The bar was one of those post-industrial conversions with exposed beams and too much attitude - equal parts cocktail lab and warehouse therapy session. Low lighting, brick walls, filament bulbs, and soft jazz-hop looping through ceiling speakers.

The chalkboard menu offered drinks with names like Celestial Sour, Adaptogen Storm, and Gut Instinct - most of which boasted ingredients Jonah either didn't recognise or actively feared.

He spotted them near the back - a cluster of work colleagues semi-circled around a high table littered with half-drunk kombuchas and a single shared plate of sweet potato crisps.

"Hey, there he is!" Elliot called, arms raised like Jonah had just returned from war.

Jonah offered a sheepish wave as he threaded through the crowd.

"Birthday boy finally made it," said Sarah, smiling wide as she leaned in for an awkward air-kiss. Her dress shimmered with some kind of cosmic pattern - planets, moons, and a five-year-olds version of a shooting star.

Terry from Finance stood next to her, sipping something cloudy from a whiskey glass.

"Can't believe you're thirty-one," he said, shaking his head. "You were supposed to self-actualise by now."

"Thirty-three...I missed the sign-up window," Jonah replied.

Terry laughed and clapped him on the back, nearly spilling his drink.

"This one's called a 'Conscious Masculine Negroni,'" Terry said proudly. "It's got zero alcohol and a hint of... shame?"

Jonah raised an eyebrow. "Sounds like my twenties."

The interns, Kai and Juniper, were deep in a conversation about breathwork retreats and ayahuasca ceremonies in Peru. They barely looked up as Jonah joined the group. One of them nodded vaguely, eyes glassy from too much Lion's Mane extract.

A few minutes later, Clarke arrived - a blast from a louder, looser past. Brash, suited, charming, loud enough to gather orbit before he reached the table. He wore his confidence like tailored armour, the kind Jonah remembered too well: pinstripes and punchlines, forged in City bars and investment floor banter, smoothed by champagne and quarterly bonuses.

His energy filled the room like a well-timed bass drop.

"Jonah Vale, you aging bastard," Clarke grinned, pulling him into a firm hug. "Still pretending to enjoy turmeric cocktails with people who don't blink?"

The Gen Z health crew looked at each other and shifted in their ergonomic seats, caught between confusion and curiosity - as if a relic from a forgotten empire had wandered in and started speaking fluent Latin.

"Only on sacred occasions," Jonah murmured.

Sarah leaned in and whispered. "Is this your friend?" As if Clarke were a performance artist gone off-script.

Jonah nodded, a little too slowly.

"You look like you need something real," Clarke said, scanning the bar. "Do they even have beer here?"

"They've got mushroom ale and sober mezcal."

"Fuck."

Clarke leaned into the bar.

"Alright, what's the closest thing you've got to a lager?" Clarke asked, squinting at the neon beer board behind the bar.

The bartender, wearing nail polish and a shirt that said *Malt Vibes Only*, didn't miss a beat.

"Probably the Emotional Support Animal. It's a Himalayan Salt & Yuzu IPA with adaptogenic mushrooms and a reiki-infused dry-hop finish."

Clarke blinked.

"Does it taste like beer?"

"Define beer."

"...Fine. One Emotional Support Animal." He turned to Jonah with a dazed look, "And a shot of - sorry I fucking asked!"

He grabbed the drink and scanned the group. Within a beat he turned his attention to Sarah. He plucked the mushroom that was wedged at the top of his beer glass, "Hungry?" He offered. She blushed and giggled.

Jonah watched them like a scene from someone else's play.

Clarke was already describing a negotiation he'd had that week - something to do with derivatives, or multi-nationals, or maybe both. Jonah wasn't really listening. He just watched the way the group leaned in. Terry blinked faster. Sarah laughed like she was hearing a foreign language she wished she'd studied. Even Elliot looked vaguely impressed.

Jonah felt it - an anti-gravity swell rising in his chest. Like the table had quietly declared him irrelevant and he was now floating inches above it, slowly drifting away. Not pulled by force but repelled by it.

Clarke was the past, slick and caffeinated. The others were the present, bright-eyed and wellness-obsessed. Jonah was... something else. A ghost in his own skin. Too jaded for the green juice, too soul-wrung for the quarterly report.

He picked at the label on his kombucha, the irony not lost on him. Fermented tea. A living drink for a life he didn't recognise.

He watched Clarke recount the deal like it was war poetry, and Sarah devour each word like gospel. And Jonah wondered, not for the first time, if the only place he truly belonged was between the lines of a story.

Maybe that's all he had left.

Maybe he should leave. Go home and write it down. Capture the absurdity of it all before it slipped through the cracks of memory like everything else.

He pictured the words:
"It was the night the old world and the new world collided, and I realised I'd been exiled from both."

Yes. That might be the start of something...

He was jolted from his reflection as Elliot gave a small toast - nothing too dramatic, just enough for social obligation.

"To Jonah," Elliot said, holding up his matcha mojito. "A man of mystery, melancholy, and... the best internal monologues in the company."

"Here, here," Sarah chimed, her eyes still lingering on Clarke.

"May this year bring him peace, pleasure, and a better espresso machine."

They clinked glasses.

He watched as someone snapped a photo of the group, digitally preserving the moment before it even mattered. He wasn't smiling in the shot. He took a sip of something vaguely herbal that left his tongue numb.

The group turned back to their splintered conversation; Elliot diving into an obscure design joke with the interns, Terry revisiting his fantasy football team for the third time, and Clarke now deep in flirtation with Sarah, who laughed too easily at everything he said.

Jonah sat quietly, swirling his glass and their voices faded to ambient noise. Their movements slowed. The room grew grainy, like film left too long in the projector.

You don't belong here anymore.

The thought came uninvited, but not unwelcome.

It was true, like a lion pacing behind the curtain.

He kept thinking about the package. About the glitch. About the weird itch in the back of his mind like someone trying to whisper through concrete.

Jonah stared into his glass again watching a single melting ice cube rotate like it was trying to escape. Around him, the noise blurred into a warm, meaningless hum.

Jonah wasn't in the conversation. Or the room. Or even, really, in his body.

He looked up.

The bartender - the one with chipped black nail polish and the *MALT VIBES ONLY* shirt - was frozen mid-pour, bottle tilted, but no liquid coming out. His face blank. Not paused. Not confused. Just… *idle*.

Like a videogame character waiting for its next command.

Then the neon sign behind the bar flickered. Twice.

The words *STAY GROUNDED* pulsed hot pink and then…
rearranged themselves.

Just for a second.

GRUNTED DAYS

Jonah blinked.
The sign flickered again. Returned to normal.

The bartender resumed pouring, as if nothing had happened.

He glanced around.

No one else had noticed.

Elliot was telling some story about an ayahuasca retreat he never actually went on. Clarke was doing shots with Sarah now. Everything was normal.

But Jonah felt it again - that vertigo of the soul. Like reality had lurched.

Jonah stood, took his coat from the back of the chair, and quietly slipped away.

No announcement.

No goodbye.

No fuss.

......

The air outside was cold and still. His breath rose in little ghosts.

Somewhere inside, the music continued playing.

He stood at the entrance for a minute, looking out. Rain clung to the air but never fully fell. Just a heavy mist that coated everything in a film of ambiguity. He felt his phone in his pocket and pulled it out. He looked at the message through his breath:

"Hey J… wasn't sure if I should text. Hope you're good. Happy Birthday. Stay weird. Sx"

Sadie; a number he should have deleted some time ago. He started walking.

He stopped in the halo of a lamppost and again looked at the screen. He typed, erased. Typed again.

"Come find out."

He hit send before he could think better of it and stuffed the phone back in his pocket. He shoved his hands into his coat pockets and kept his eyes down; shoulders hunched against nothing in particular and started towards home.

The Package.

When he entered his apartment, the smell hit him first - something between stale takeout and damp socks. The weak street light filtering through the windows gave it an air of ambient chaos - a random storage space; somewhere lived in but not loved.

He flicked on the lights, flinched at the brightness, then stood there for a moment just looking.

His phone pinged.

"You silver tongued devil…how can a girl resist huh? Sxx"

"Shit."

He hadn't expected her to reply, let alone show up. He looked at his apartment through her hypothetical eyes.

"Shit…shit….shit."

He darted forward, grabbing a tea towel and batting at the mess like it might vanish if he moved fast enough. He ran around, collecting armfuls of discarded clothes which he pushed into the bottom of his wardrobe and forced the doors closed. He collected takeout boxes and empty cups that he hung from his fingers and ran into the kitchen. It was a war zone; more takeout boxes, unwashed dishes, a rogue sock draped over a blender. Panic flared in his chest like a smoke alarm going off.

That's when he noticed it; the package.

Still nestled in the forest of coffee cups on the dining table, exactly where he'd thrown it that morning.

His breath caught and he forgot the kitchen.

It was plain, hand-wrapped in rough brown paper. No barcode. No branding. No postage stamp. Just his name, written in looping black ink across the front: *Jonah Vale.*

Who writes things by hand now, he thought.

It was warm when he picked it up.

Heavy.

Heavier than it looked. Not physically, but… *energetically.* Like it carried something old. Something dense. Something that had waited a long time.

He sat on a dining chair and cleared a small area to set it down carefully. It was tied with a coarse, thick twine; a neat bow held it together. He pulled at the twine and the package opened like a fist relaxing its grip.

It was a book. No. A journal.

Leather-bound, worn smooth by time and touch. Deep mahogany in colour, etched with a strange symbol - a single spiral, that instead of continuing smoothly to the centre, stops abruptly and transforms into a straight line that cuts outward. It shimmered faintly under the light, even though it wasn't metallic.

For a moment, he just stared at it. He *knew* this book. Something nostalgic pulled deep in his gut as if he'd just remembered a promise he'd made and forgotten a long time ago. He felt the air thicken around him, and his senses became hyper-vigilant. He'd tried Ecstasy once, and he remembers how everything slowed like thick air, and he disappeared headlong into the details of everything around him: the weave of his trousers, the movement and sound of his watch, his own body odour.

He became acutely aware of his own breath. The room felt wrong. Too quiet. The fridge hum seemed to pulse in waves. The lights flickered, or maybe it was just his vision.

He reached out and touched the cover. He traced the spiral of the glyph with his fingertip. A subtle vibration thrummed up through his wrists from the package, like a distant drumbeat played through the bones of the earth - it travelled up his arms and into his chest. He felt his heartbeat synchronise with the deep beat.

Primal.
Familiar.
Wrongly placed in time.

He felt a jolt - like a tuning fork inside his ribcage had been struck after decades of silence.

What the hell is this?

His fingers trembled as he opened the cover.

No title. No preface. No instructions.

Just page after page of hand-drawn symbols: lines, curves, spirals, stars, glyphs - none of them recognizable, yet all of them inexplicably intimate. As if his body remembered what his mind did not.

The ink shimmered faintly, reacting to the movement of his eyes.

A strange ache spread across his chest. Not pain. Not fear.

A deep, soul-level nostalgia. The kind of longing that had no language.

Each page pulsed with meaning he couldn't grasp. Like reading the dreams of a past life he'd barely survived.

He flipped through more pages, heart hammering, breathing shallow. Most were filled with the symbols, some were blank, as if waiting for a new author.

And then…

A voice.

Not spoken aloud. Not even heard. Just felt, deep in the marrow.

"You are beginning to see."

He stared at the page, lips parted.

Was it in the ink?

Was it in him?

The symbols rearranged themselves. One of them burned for a second - a five pointed star, with what looked like an eye in the centre, and then...

A knock at the door.

He flinched, slammed the journal shut like he'd been caught with something illegal and stumbled to his feet.

Another knock - playful, rhythmic.

He zig-zagged through the living room and opened the door. There stood Sadie, fringe swept sideways, eyeliner smudged in deliberate rebellion, dressed for fun. That grin; mischief and memory. She raised one brow and held up two items like a sacred offering:

"I brought gifts."

In one hand: a pair of fluffy pink handcuffs.

In the other - a small silver pouch labelled Golden Teachers.

"You said to come find out."

Jonah laughed - a genuine sound, released without thought. He stepped aside, and she slipped in like a returning storm. Once inside she paused and looked at the apartment.

"I like what you've done with the place." Jonah grimaced, but she winked and threw her arms around his neck.

Her mouth found his and she kissed him deep. His mouth, teeth, were resistant at first; like an animal trap that had sprung shut. The vulnerability was unfamiliar, then he yielded to the insistence of her tongue. With the release, he forgot everything; the mess, the journal, the internal ache. A low groan vibrated deep in his throat, his primal masculine, released from the trap he'd carefully cultivated. He pushed her backwards onto the cluttered couch, and they spiralled together, a tangle of limbs and tainted memories.

The night blurred in fragments. The kitchen still a mess. The journal still closed.

They sat in the afterglow. An unspoken agreement pulsed between them that they had enjoyed each other for their own reasons, which didn't matter right now. In this moment.

Sadie sat cross-legged on the floor, tearing open the silver pouch with a familiar chaos. The scent of earth and citrus wafted out - mushrooms, wrapped in wax paper like some illicit pastry.

"You always did like your sacraments fermented," she said with a wink, popping one into her mouth. "Want in?"

Jonah didn't answer.

He was nested in the corner of the sofa; arms folded lightly across his chest. The journal sat just out of sight, but not out of *mind* - its gravity pulling at the edge of his attention now that his relief valve had popped.

Sadie looked up.

"You're quieter than usual. Which is saying something. Usually I have to break you open like a fortune cookie."

Jonah managed a thin smile. But it cracked fast.

"Do you ever feel like… everything's off?" he said quietly. "Like the world's wearing the wrong skin?"

Sadie blinked. Chewed. Swallowed.

"All the time. It's called capitalism."

"No. I mean… deeper. Like… this isn't *real.*"

There was silence for a moment. Not avoidance - just a soft pocket of space where truth could safely land.

Sadie leaned in a little closer. Attentive, interested.

"Go on, you can tell me. I've seen your worst hair days. I've earned this." She smiled softly.

41

Jonah exhaled.

Sadie didn't push, she just reached for his hand, unthreading his arms with a tenderness that caught him off guard. Her fingers were warm, familiar, annoyingly grounding.

"Hey," she said gently, "I've seen you spiral over oat milk brands. This feels…bigger."

He let out something between a laugh and a breath, but it was brittle - like glass worn thin.

"It's like…" he started, then paused. "Like there's this… low hum. All the time. Like something's wrong with the engine but no one else hears it. Everyone just keeps driving."

Sadie tilted her head, watching him.

"But you hear it?"

"I *feel* it," he said. "In my teeth. In my chest. Like I'm waiting for something that already happened, and I missed it. Or forgot it. And now I'm stuck pretending I know the lines to a play I never auditioned for."

She spoke softly, "you're talking like someone who forgot they have a body."

He stared at her. So open. So effortless. Like she wasn't haunted by the same ache. Like she didn't lie awake at night, wondering what the hell this whole thing was about.

"Maybe I did," he said, smiling weakly.

"Then maybe it's time to *get back in*." Her eyes twinkled slightly.

From the paper bag beside her, she pulled another mushroom - smaller than the others, misshapen like it had grown sideways in the dark. She held it up between her fingers.

"Here. For presence. Not for answers."

He hesitated, the buzz of the journal still somewhere behind him, humming like a broken memory.

Sadie leaned forward and popped the mushroom gently into his mouth.

"Chew," she whispered.

He did.

Bitter. Earthy. Sharp.

He swallowed.

She smiled and stood up, padding across the living room in her stockinged feet. Jonah, sprawled on the couch, half-naked and grinning, watched her from a distance.

'This?" she asked, holding up the journal.

"Yeah…that's it - something I found. Might be cursed."

She flipped through a few pages.

Her nose wrinkled.

"Weird symbols. No plot."

She tossed it onto the couch like it was a mildly disappointing art book.

"Not my thing."

It fell open on a blank page.

"Figures," Jonah murmured. She came and wrapped herself in him.

"Sometimes," she said, brushing his hair back with slow fingers, "stepping into the unknown is the only honest answer we have."

Jonah looked at her - really looked. And for a brief, shimmering second, her face blurred at the edges. Like she didn't quite belong to this world. Or maybe like he didn't.

Then she laughed - full, unapologetic - and pulled him down to the floor beside her.

And just like that, the ache in his chest dissolved into heat. His breath deepened. The edges of his thoughts softened. And the weight he always carried quietly slipped into the corner, still watching, but no longer in control.

She slid her hand down the crack of the sofa and pulled out the handcuffs. She dangled them on a crooked finger and mischievously nodded her head towards the bedroom.

The Room that wasn't there.

It was raining inside the house.

Jonah stood barefoot in the hallway of his childhood home, and the ceiling dripped like it was crying through its seams.

Everything was muted sepia, as though memory had been water damaged. The wallpaper was peeling in floral strips. A hallway stretched further than it should. Shadows bent the corners.

Hands on hips. Lipsticked smile stretched thin and sour, he saw his mother.

He heard her voice, sharp and sweet.

"Look at this mess," she hissed. "Always leaving crumbs. Always making me clean up after you."

Jonah looked down.

There were no crumbs.

The floor was spotless. Sterile.

Still, she advanced, her presence heavy, angular. She was flickering like an old film reel - cleaning dishes that bled light as she walked.

"I told you to be a good boy. Good boys don't cause trouble. Good boys don't ask questions. Good boys don't *see* things."

She leaned in, her breath like rusted perfume.

"Do you understand me, Jonah?"

He tried to speak, but his voice caught - his mouth filled with cotton, his throat a locked door.

Now she loomed over him - faceless, her back was stiff. Her voice echoed even though she was right upon him.

"Not now, Jonah. Mummy's busy. Go play."

The wallpaper behind her began to ripple. Symbols emerged - *the same as the journal*. Spirals. Glyphs. An alphabet of a world he hadn't yet earned the right to read.

Her eyes glowed with something metallic. Not rage. Not sorrow.

Suppression.

"Stop digging," she whispered. "You don't want to know what's beneath."

He turned and ran - feet moving without sound, the hallway stretching impossibly long.

At the end, a door stood where no door had ever been. Carved with strange symbols. Warm to the touch.

He opened it.

Inside: a man, cross-legged on the floor, surrounded by orbs of hovering light. His face was familiar - too familiar.

"Your father," said a voice he couldn't place, just behind his left shoulder.

The man turned and smiled.

"You made it back. Good. It's almost time to leave again."

Jonah opened his mouth to speak but nothing came. Only wind.

The lights dimmed. The orbs cracked like eggshells, spilling galaxies. His father leaned in and whispered something into his ear.

Jonah couldn't hear it.

Only feel it. Like a symbol pressed into the flesh of his soul.

And then…

The far wall opened.

Like a curtain being drawn from the inside.

And Jonah saw it.

The Veil

It wasn't a place.

It was a structure - interwoven light and static, a lattice of thought and energy stretching across the sky like a web spun from silence. Behind it, strange shapes moved: vast forms, pulsing with hunger. *The Greys.* Not with faces - just *presences.* They siphoned light, coiled around symbols, fed on something he couldn't name.

The Veil pulsed with purpose.

He felt it more than saw it: an energetic net cast over minds, distorting reality, suppressing truth. It moved through bureaucracy, through pharmaceuticals, through apps promising calm while planting cages.

He saw people.

Billions of them.

Sleeping with eyes open. Marching. Nodding. Smiling in photographs taken inside their own prisons.

And then - he saw himself.

Awake. On fire. *Burning through the net.*

But only for a second.

The vision cracked like glass.

49

….

Jonah gasped awake.

Chest heaving. Skin slick with sweat.

The apartment was dark, the only light came squeezing through the blinds from the street. Sadie snored softly beside him, wrapped in the duvet like a child, her hair fanned across his pillow like ink spilled in reverse.

He caught his breath and blinked. The mould-eye on the ceiling pulsed like it was watching, waiting to see what would happen next.

He sat up.

Put his feet on the floor.

His hands trembled.

The words his father whispered echoed in the back of his skull, but no matter how hard he tried to recall them, they slipped further away.

Still, something was different now.

He had seen it.

Even if he didn't understand.

Not yet.

Like the ache that lived under his skin had a name now. And it was beginning to wake.

He walked through the living room and looked around in the half-light; the apartment was a shipwreck. Crumpled clothes draped over chairs like abandoned sails. An open pizza box sagged on the coffee table, its contents congealing in the dawn light. He headed towards the bathroom then paused as he saw the journal, lay on the couch where they had left it the night before. The page he had left blank the night before now had writing on it.

It simply said:

"Go back to the room. He's still waiting."

Jonah stared at it, heart hammering. He ran his fingers over the ink. It was dry. Firm. Real.

His head throbbed with that dull, hollow ache that always followed nights like this. He grunted as he pushed open the bathroom door, already shielding his eyes from the sudden brightness to come.

Reaching upward, his fingers grasped at empty air.

He blinked. Stared up at the ceiling.

No cord.

He frowned and looked to the side.

There, by the doorframe - a sleek, modern wall switch, embedded cleanly into the tile. Smooth white plastic.

"What the...?"

He pressed it, and the light came on instantly - bright, clean, clinical.

He just stood there, blinking under its glare. The memory of the cord - his hand tugging it just yesterday - wasn't a dream. He was sure of it. As sure as he was that the toothpaste cap never made it back on, and the mirror fogged unevenly.

He stood there for a moment longer, staring at the switch as if it might confess something.

He walked back into the bedroom, head spinning, needing to share. He sat on the bed next to Sadie.

"Hey..." he shook her gently, but she twisted herself further into the covers and turned away. With a small shake of his head, he went back to the bathroom. He quickly showered and brushed his teeth in silence. He looked in his cupboard and found nothing hanging, just the pile he'd hastily rammed in earlier. He picked some out and sniffed them, selecting the least crumpled. He pulled a piece of paper from his nightstand and wrote Sadie a note, gently placing it on the bed. He kissed her on the head before he left.

He slid his laptop into his work bag, then pausing, he walked back and plucked the journal from the sofa. He pushed it into his bag and headed for the door. By some small miracle, Bessie was on the right floor and he shuddered down the lift, glassy eyed.

In the Lobby was Graham, mopping the floor again.

"Mornin', Jonah," he called without looking up. "Rough one?"

"Yeah, you could say that." He looked a bit sheepish. "You know, um…"

Graham winks "Yeah, I know. Sadie. Saw her come through last night. Nice girl, interesting taste in jewellery…all fluffy like." He indicates the handcuffs.

Jonah blinks at him, "Just makes sure she gets…you know…"

"Sure thing Jonah, I'll see her safely out, get her into a cab. As long as you've not left her, you know, chained to a radiator or something." He chuckled to himself and shook his head.

Jonah's mind was elsewhere. "Listen… has anyone been in my flat lately?"

Graham stopped mopping, leaned on the handle like it was a staff of office. Behind him, Janice, his wife, stepped out from their apartment. She'd been listening.

"Into your flat?" She gave a humourless laugh. "Nobody's brave enough for that. Looks like the aftermath of a poltergeist binge in there."

Jonah managed a thin smile.

"No, I mean - maintenance. You know, anyone change out fixtures or... switch stuff up?"

Graham raised an eyebrow.

"Fixtures? Nah. We barely have budget for new bulbs in the hallway."

Janice chipped in, "Why? Something wrong?"

Jonah looked back toward the lift, as if the strange switch might be staring down at him from behind the doors.

"No. Nothing wrong. Just… odd."

"Could've been you in a drunken DIY frenzy," Graham grinned. "Maybe you're the handyman you've been waiting for." He did a wooo noise.

"Yeah," Jonah said, distracted. "Maybe." He nodded to them both and turned.

He stepped out onto the street, the city yawning around him like it always had. But something in his chest felt… out of place. As if reality had tilted slightly, and everyone else had simply learned to walk sideways.

The Loop.

The office elevator hummed with the sterile quiet of early arrivals. The kind of silence that hadn't yet been caffeinated into small talk. Jonah stepped off on the fifth floor and was greeted by the familiar smells: sandalwood air freshener, turmeric energy bites, and printer toner.

He walked into the open space like a stranger in his own life.

Elliot was walking across the floor, first coffee in hand and nodded. He looked pale. A little more subdued than usual.

"You ghosted last night," he said.

Jonah shrugged, dropping his bag.

"Wasn't feeling it."

He moved in closer on his way past, "Clarke and Sarah were still at it when I left. Pretty sure they didn't even notice you were gone."

Jonah looked over. Sarah, caught his eye and immediately turned away, her cheeks tinged red. She busied herself with a smoothie bottle and something that may or may not have been a guilt complex.

Elliot shrugged and continued his slow walk to his desk.

Kai and Juniper, the interns, walked past looking like they'd just emerged from a failed breathwork ceremony. Sunglasses indoors. Sipping green sludge like it contained penance.

Jonah didn't sit but headed straight for the coffee station. Back at his desk, he sat and tried to shake the heaviness in his limbs. He reached into his bag and placed the journal on his desk; dull, heavy, undeniable. As it landed with a thud, the banana Buddha twitched next to his monitor. He looked at the two items side by side and thought; *ancient cosmic cipher, meet commercial enlightenment.* He snorted and shook his head.

"This is my life now." He muttered.

His screen had returned to normal after yesterday's incident - a flicker of symbols, unreadable yet somehow familiar, dancing across his desktop for just a second before vanishing. IT had chalked it up to a corrupt extension or a background update.

Jonah wasn't so sure.

As he stared blankly at his blinking cursor that refused to focus, a voice cut across the open-plan blur:

"Hey, did you see the sky this morning? Looked painted."

He looked up.

Terry was leaning on the divider between their desks, grinning over the rim of his mug which said; *Worlds Okayest Accountant*. Always the early bird. Always vaguely damp from the cycle in. Friendly in that performative, office-appropriate way. As he grinned, the banana Buddha sprang to life:

"You are light. You are flow. You are the harmony between breath and spreadsheet."

The two of them looked at it in surprise. It was too surreal to comment.

"Painted?" Jonah said, blinking and dragging his gaze back to Terry. "No. I didn't even look up."

Terry chuckled. "Shame. Whole sky looked like someone spilled oil on a mirror."

Jonah smirked. "You always see weird shit in the sky, Terry."

"Weird shit?" Terry looked at Jonah, then at the Buddha. "Yeah…whatever." Terry gave a wink and ambled off toward the printer. As he disappeared, "I like to think of it as being observant, mate."

Jonah turned back to his screen, stared at the insistent cursor like it was mocking him. His fingers hovered above the keyboard, then slowly settled.

Then…

"Hey, did you see the sky this morning? Looked painted."

Jonah felt a jolt through is body and his blood chilled.

He turned. Terry was back - same stance, same coffee mug, same grin.

Jonah stared at him. "You just said that," he said.

Terry blinked. "Said what?"

The Buddha started up again…"*You are light. You are flow…*"Jonah grabbed the thing around the head and shook it to stop the voice, "*You are the harmony between breath and…*" Jonah stuffed it head down, buried deep in the soil of the rubber plant. Terry watched the performance, open mouthed. Jonah turned back, irritated.

"About the sky. The oil and mirror thing."

Terry took a beat to recover. "I didn't say anything, mate," he dragged his eyes back to Jonah from the semi-buried Buddha. "But… *weird* you mention it. Did you see it? Looked wild this morning."

Jonah stared at him. Hard.

Everything looked… identical. Same mug. Same lean. Even the rhythm of his sentence felt copy-pasted.

"You're messing with me," Jonah muttered.

"Me?" He looked slightly confused for a second, "Haven't had enough coffee to mess with anyone," Terry hesitated. "You alright? You look like you saw a ghost."

Jonah forced a laugh, leaned back in his chair.

"No, I'm good. Just - long night."

"Fair enough," Terry said, already walking away again. "Sky's still there, either way."

Jonah waited a full minute before turning back to his screen.

It looked normal.

But in the top right corner of his monitor - just above the time readout - something flickered. A symbol. A spiral. Brief. Gone. The journal sat next to him, humming in his peripheral vision, even closed. He didn't dare touch it yet.

Team Building

At 10am, River called everyone into the conference room, which had been transformed overnight into a creativity dojo. It was a team building exercise and everyone filed in.

Colourful art supplies covered the long central table: glue sticks, foam blocks, metallic pipe cleaners, glitter pens, modelling clay, googly eyes, pom-poms, neon sticky notes, biodegradable glitter, ethically-sourced feathers. It looked like a unicorn had exploded.

Jonah sat alone, slightly distracted. Elliot dropped into the seat beside him, peeling open a granola bar like it owed him money.

"Something up?" he asked, mouth full.

Jonah leaned closer, voice low.

"Have you noticed Terry acting weird lately?"

"Terry's always weird," Elliot said with a laugh. "He's like a sentient dad joke. Guy has two modes: football commentary and random weather observations. You could replace him with a screensaver, and no one would notice."

Jonah didn't laugh.

At the end of the long table stood River.

"Okay, team!" she chirped, clapping her hands like a sunrise in human form. "Today is all about *vision*! The future we want to create, not just for ourselves, but for the world."

Jonah winced.

River gestured toward the art supply buffet.

"Build something - anything - that captures your vision of the future. What you want to grow. Where you want to go. What you want to *become*."

She smiled like this was the most profound thing anyone had ever said.

Jonah sank a little lower in his chair and he and Elliot looked at each other. Elliot shrugged his shoulders, mouthed: "Kill me slowly." He disposed of his granola wrapper and dove in.

Everyone got to work, each claiming a space somewhere at the edge of the room. Jonah hunkered in a corner and took a deep breath. In a half-trancelike state, he reached for the words his father had whispered in his dream last night. It was as if they were just teetering on the edge of his consciousness. They felt important, yet he just couldn't get them into form. His heart hammered as he pictured the vision he'd seen; and his hands worked on their own.

Half an hour later, River clapped her hands enthusiastically and brought everybody back together.

First up were Kai and Juniper, who had worked together and had crafted a bridge made from popsicle sticks and rainbow yarn, labelling it *"Connection."*

Sarah made a tree out of green clay and wire, with glittery roots and star-shaped leaves. She called it *"Reach."*

Elliot built a tower out of foam bricks with mirrors glued to each side. *"Infinite Potential,"* he said, and the room clapped like it was church.

River beamed.

"Incredible. You're all *so* tuned in today. Jonah, you're up next!"

Jonah hadn't moved for most of the session. But now, he stood slowly.

"Yeah. Okay."

He stepped aside to reveal his creation, which he'd hidden behind a screen of cardboard.

It wasn't pretty.

It was *too* precise. Too stark.

A cage - delicately woven from pipe cleaners and wooden skewers - loomed over a small human figure made of clay, faceless and curled in on itself. Above it, spirals of black thread wove a dense net, covered in sharp glyph-like etchings drawn in permanent marker. There was a gleaming white orb suspended above it all - brilliant, but unreachable, wrapped in coils of copper wire.

Silence fell over the room like a curtain.

River's smile froze in place.

Elliot's eyebrows lifted slowly.

The interns looked physically nauseous.

Terry leaned back in his chair, arms folded, as if this confirmed something he'd suspected all along.

Sarah burst out laughing - short, shrill, and uncontrollable. It echoed too loud in the quiet.

"Jonah..." River said gently. "Do you want to, uh, walk us through what we're seeing?"

Jonah's voice came low. Steady. But with that edge - the one that says something long trapped is finally breathing air.

"This," he said, gesturing to the structure, "is the story we sell. Wellness. Growth. Expansion. A curated life, hand-picked for perfection."

He pointed to the cage.

"But this is what it really is. A loop. A gilded repetition. All our rituals and routines, our supplements and visualisations and quantified self-improvement - they're *bars*."

A pause.

"We call it progress. But it's performance. Controlled freedom. Safe rebellion. A beautiful prison built from our own stories."

No one moved.

Jonah stared at his sculpture.

Then he looked at the team.

"This morning, I thought maybe I was losing it. But now? I think this…" he jabbed a finger at the cage, "…this is what makes us forget who we are."

He took a breath, met River's horrified-but-still-trying eyes.

"And I'm done pretending it's enough."

Then he turned.

And walked out the door.

The Meeting

The building door swung shut behind him with a finality that sounded like a sentence. Not a word. Not a goodbye. A *verdict*.

Jonah stepped into the street and was swallowed by the indifferent rhythm of the city.

Feet moved around him. Horns honked in the distance. Phones buzzed. The machine of modern life churned on, utterly unaffected by the fact that he had just walked out of his job - his salary, his routine, his safety net - and had nothing waiting on the other side.

He clutched the journal to his chest like a stolen artifact.

What the fuck did I just do?

The question rattled through his skull with every step.

He passed a vegan taco van. The smell made his stomach turn. A poster flashed on a glass building - *Meditation for Executives: Awaken Your Inner CEO*. A bus rumbled past with an ad for serotonin-enhancing toothpaste. Someone banged into his shoulder and didn't apologise.

Where am I going?

He didn't know.

He just kept walking.

He thought about calling Sadie. Just hearing her voice. Just pretending, for a moment, that the old world was still intact. She may even still be in his flat from last night. He looked at his watch, *unlikely* he thought.

His hand hovered over his phone.

Then pulled back.

No.

She was part of the lie. Even if she didn't mean to be. Even if she *wanted* to understand.

So, who do I turn to?

No one. There was no one.

He was in the wasteland now.

He walked for what felt like a number of hours. The rhythm gave him a sense of making some kind of progress, even though he had no idea where he was going. He eventually ended up at the edge of a park in a part of town he had never been; half-forgotten and gently decaying, tucked between two high-rises that looked like glass mausoleums. The bench he sat on creaked under his weight. The journal rested on his knees.

He stared at nothing. His mind had shut down; overwhelmed with too many questions for which he couldn't answer.

The wind moved through the trees with a whispering sound, like old gods mumbling through leaves. Familiar, calling him back. He closed his eyes and tried to gather his thoughts; chastising himself for not being able to solve his problems.

"That's quite a heavy thing you're carrying."

Jonah opened his eyes again and looked up.

A man stood in front of him. Mid-forties, maybe. Elegant in a way that didn't try. Long green coat, collar slightly turned, a dark feather tucked into one lapel. His hair was slicked back but not fussed over. Calm eyes. Blue, but not cold. He looked like he belonged somewhere - but not *here*.

"Excuse me?" Jonah said.

The man nodded toward the journal.

"That book. It hums. Not everyone hears it, but when they do… it usually means something's cracked open."

Jonah blinked.

"How do you know about the book?"

The man smiled - gently, like he wasn't surprised by the question.

"Because I had one once. Different shape. Same weight."

Jonah gripped the journal a little tighter. The edge between paranoia and recognition was razor-thin.

"Who are you?"

The man stepped closer, not invading, but inhabiting space with an ease Jonah appreciated.

"My name is Lucien. And I'm someone who's made the same leap you just did."

Jonah stared at him, frowning.

"You saw what I made in there?"

Lucien shook his head.

"Didn't have to. I *felt* it. That kind of rupture leaves a trace in the field. You just tore a hole in your own narrative. That's not small."

Jonah lowered his gaze.

Lucien glanced at the empty space beside Jonah on the bench, then took a seat without asking. He didn't speak at first - just looked out across the park, as if watching something move between the trees that only he could see.

"It's like this," he said finally, his tone soft, measured. "Most people spend their whole lives patching the cracks in their stories. You… let yours split open."

Jonah turned to him, wary.

"You don't even know me."

Lucien smiled faintly. "I know what it feels like to suffocate behind a version of yourself that was never yours to begin with."

The words landed somewhere deep in Jonah's chest - sharp and disarming, like someone had just found the thing he'd been hiding, named it, and offered it back without judgment.

Lucien met his gaze.

"When you rip the scab off, it's messy at first. Always is."

There was a long pause. Something in Jonah softened - not quite trust, but the exhaustion of holding it all in.

"I don't even know why I did it," Jonah said quietly. "I just… couldn't lie anymore."

Lucien nodded with a softness that felt undeserved.

"Most people can't articulate it. That ache. That gnawing sense that reality is *off* - like we're all performing in a play that never had a writer. Many people reach the edge, but most don't leap. You've done what most people can't.' He smiled with his eyes, deep and full of understanding. 'You're not crazy. You're *awakening*."

Jonah's throat tightened.

"Yeah," he whispered. "But awakening to *what?*"

Lucien tilted his head. His eyes held a flicker of something - compassion, sure, but also curiosity. Like Jonah was a puzzle he was delighted to see finally taken out of the box.

"That's not for me to answer," Lucien said. "But…" He drew out the pause, "you don't have to do this alone."

Jonah felt tears press at the back of his eyes, unexpected and hot.

"I thought I was." His voice cracked slightly.

Lucien sat beside him, like they'd always sat here, on this particular bench, waiting for this very moment.

"You were. Until just now."

He let that crack open a little wider; allowed the silence to feed it.

Jonah just nodded slightly. If he used it, he didn't trust his voice would hold back the flood; a flimsy dam of sticks containing a mighty reservoir. A single tear wound its way through a crack, down his cheek. He felt a little cool relief as a soft rain started to fall through the trees.

Lucien gave him a meaningful smile. "Coffee?"

The coffee shop was quiet in that afternoon lull - just the soft hum of a milk steamer, the occasional clink of cups, and the rain's gentle percussion against the wide glass windows. Jonah sat opposite the stranger he'd just met in the park, and somehow, it didn't feel strange at all. There was something about Lucien - his calmness, his stillness - that made Jonah feel like he'd stepped outside the noise of his own life for the first time in years.

Lucien stirred his espresso slowly, like he was measuring time in spirals.

Jonah exhaled and shook his head. "I don't know what I'm doing. I've just walked out. Again." His voice cracked at the edge. "Left a job that people would kill for. And for what? No plan. No next step. Just... nothing."

Lucien smiled, not with amusement, but with a kind of knowing. "That's not nothing, Jonah. That's everything."

Jonah blinked. "It doesn't feel like everything. It feels like I've ruined my life. Again."

"You haven't ruined anything," Lucien said gently, leaning in. "You've simply outgrown what was never meant for you. That's the pain of conscious evolution - it doesn't come with a blueprint. It comes with a rupture."

Jonah looked down at his chipped mug of tea. "Maybe it's just me. My mother always said I was good at starting things. Not so good at seeing them through. That I want too much. That I don't live in the real world. Maybe she's right."

Lucien's gaze didn't waver. "That's because the 'real world' she's referring to is a construct. A beautifully maintained cage. Most people don't realise they're in it. You've realised it. That makes you dangerous."

Jonah let the words sit. Dangerous? He'd never thought of himself that way. Just lost. Scraping by. A boy in a man's body, carrying a journal like a confession he couldn't read.

Lucien reached into the satchel at his side and pulled out a notebook. The leather was worn and supple. He placed it gently on the table and opened it. Symbols. Diagrams. Strange glyphs that looked like they'd been pulled from the seams of a dream.

Jonah's breath caught. "That's… That's like mine."

Lucien nodded. "Of course. These things don't arrive by accident. They're markers. Breadcrumbs for those willing to follow."

Jonah touched his own jacket pocket, where the weight of the journal sat like a small, persistent heartbeat. "I thought I was losing it," he said. "Seeing things. Feeling things. It's like I'm haunted by something I don't understand."

"You're not haunted," Lucien said. "You're being called. There's a difference."

Jonah sat back, suddenly lighter. The ache that had lived beneath his ribs for as long as he could remember - like a sleeping creature curled around his soul - seemed to loosen its grip.

"What if I'm not strong enough?" he asked, his voice barely audible.

Lucien didn't flinch. "That's not your question to answer. Your job is to step forward. The strength will meet you there. It always does."

A pause hung between them. Not awkward - reverent.

Jonah looked out the window. The rain had stopped. The world glistened. Nothing had changed. And yet, everything had.

The warmth of the coffee cupped in his hands was suddenly more than warmth. It was permission. To stop spiralling. To stop searching. To stop pretending he had it all under control.

Lucien's words still echoed inside him - not as answers, but as balm. Jonah didn't quite understand how this stranger knew what he knew. How he could reach so precisely into the knots of his inner world. But he didn't push. Didn't ask.

Because the truth was - he didn't want to know.

Not yet.

Something in him was afraid that if he poked too hard at Lucien's certainty, the whole thing might dissolve. And right now, the illusion of being seen - truly seen - felt better than the pain of staying lost.

So, he let it be. Let Lucien's smooth, quiet confidence become his anchor.

Maybe this was what relief looked like.

Maybe this was what it felt like to stop holding it all alone.

"You're not alone anymore," Lucien added softly, as if plucking the thought from Jonah's mind. "There are others. There's a path."

For the first time in a long time, Jonah didn't feel like he was slipping beneath the surface. He felt anchored. Seen.

His mother's voice faded. The inner critic grew silent. The unanswered questions still hovered, but they no longer screamed.

Lucien reached out and closed his notebook. "You don't have to understand it all now," he said. "You just have to keep going. The map unfolds with movement."

Jonah nodded, slowly. "I think I needed to hear this more than anything."

Lucien smiled again. "That's how you know it's true."

Jonah absorbed that and lifted his journal onto the table.

"You've touched the source," Lucien said. "But you need help decoding it." He tapped a finger on the cover of the journal. "Otherwise, they'll get to you first."

Jonah frowned. "Who's they?"

Lucien just smiled, tapped his temple, and said:

"The ones who taught you to forget. The ones who own your fear."

Jonah didn't understand, but then, there was so much he didn't understand, and he let it go.

"We run retreats.' Said Lucien. 'There are more people like us. Think about it…You'll understand more there."

He leant forward and gave Jonah a card. He took it with both hands and looked at it. On one side, there was a spiral with the line cutting out from the centre…like on his journal. Above the spiral was an opening eye. Lucien saw his surprise.

"You think you're the only one this is happening to?" Lucien laughed lightly. "You're late to the party."

Jonah looked up from the card.

75

"Why are you helping me?"

Lucien stood, brushing something invisible off his coat sleeve.

"Because someone once helped me. And because I remember what it's like to stand where you're standing, asking the questions no one else will let themselves ask."

He stepped backward.

"You're not broken, Jonah. You're just finally refusing to forget."

And with that, he walked away - disappearing into the crowd like a ripple swallowed by still water.

Jonah sat frozen.

The journal on the table in front of him.

The card in his hand.

And for the first time in days, the ache in his chest didn't feel like death.

It felt like beginning.

The Return to the Cave

Jonah didn't go back to work. Not the next day. Not the one after that.

He ignored Elliot's texts – *"Mate, River's freaking out. Are you okay? Like, hospital okay?"* - and deleted two calendar invites that somehow still appeared on his phone despite him being logged out of every platform.

And curiously, the sky hadn't fallen.

River had left two increasingly concerned voicemails. Even Sarah from design had sent a "Hope you're okay?" text, followed by a GIF of a cartoon rabbit collapsing onto a desk with a coffee the size of its torso. He hadn't replied. Not out of rudeness, but because he didn't know how to say. *I'm not okay, but I'm closer to something that is.*

He was drifting - but it no longer felt like drowning.

Instead, he wandered.

Most mornings, he stayed in bed longer than he should have. He drank his coffee slowly, watched light slant across the floorboards like a quiet omen. And then he wrote.

Not for anyone. Not for a campaign brief or product launch. Just for himself.

At first, even opening the journal had felt like trespass. The pages had carried a weight, as if they were meant to be looked at, not written in - as though his own words might contaminate whatever strange intelligence already lived there. But eventually the pressure to speak back grew too strong.

When his pen finally touched the paper, it was with a hesitant reverence. And then, somehow, the words flowed. The journal that once felt alien now moved beneath his hand like a familiar landscape. Pages filled with fragments, symbols, strange echoes of dreams that refused to fade. And more than that: impressions. Shapes that left a tingle in his chest as if they'd carved new grooves in his mind.

One shape kept returning, unbidden. A star, but inside it - an eye. At least that's what it looked like to him. Sometimes it appeared in the margins, sometimes at the centre of a page, drawn before he realised his hand was moving. He couldn't say why he kept sketching it, only that whenever it appeared, something stirred at the back of his skull, a sense of being watched - or remembered.

He didn't understand any of it, not yet - but he felt himself being read as much as he was reading. As if the marks were less drawings and more *instructions*, pressing themselves into him, reorganising something beneath the surface.

But also - thoughts. Feelings. Pieces of himself he hadn't made space for in years.

"I don't know what this is yet," he wrote one morning, letters wavering under his hand. "But it feels like being held in a language I don't understand, but desperately need to."

Lucien had become a fixture in his days. They'd met up again that same week - another quiet café, another long conversation that felt less like being spoken to and more like being remembered.

Lucien never pressured. He never told Jonah what to do. He asked good questions. He listened. And he offered Jonah something he hadn't experienced in so long it felt mythic: stillness.

"You're not broken," he had said, over a lukewarm cortado. "You're just waking up in a world that profits from your sleep."

There was no condescension in his tone. Just gentle clarity. Like he'd walked this path himself.

Jonah found himself repeating Lucien's words in the shower, on the bus, as he stirred lentils over the stove. He'd taken to copying snippets of their conversations into the margins of his journal.

"Not all who wander are lost," he'd scribbled beside a drawing of a spiral. *"But some of us have to get lost before we can wander."*

Lucien had invited him to a retreat - *"Nothing formal,"* he said, *"Just a gathering of like-minded seekers. People like you."* Jonah had hesitated, but Lucien's calm was magnetic. *"It's not about fixing you,"* he'd added. *"It's about remembering who you were before the forgetting."*

The words landed like gospel.

Jonah had said yes.

The retreat was only a few days away, and already Jonah felt his internal tectonic plates shifting. Not violently - but with the deep creak of something old making room for something true.

He'd taken long walks. Read strange books. Slept at odd hours. The ache in his chest - once a constant companion - now flickered. Sometimes gone entirely, like a ghost finally taking the hint.

The city, once familiar, now felt like a cipher. Layers beneath layers. Messages beneath messages. And he'd begun to notice things.

Repeating numbers - 11:11, 333, 404 - on clocks, bus routes, receipt totals.

Songs that echoed his thoughts playing in cafés he'd never entered before.

He was sitting in a park again - different bench, same stare-into-space posture - when his phone rang.

It was his mother.

The name flashed on screen like a summons from an old life. His stomach tightened reflexively, as though a child had taken the call instead of the man he now tried to be.

He let it ring once. Twice. Three times. Then he picked up.

"Jonah?" came the voice.

That single word dropped into his stomach like lead.

"Hi," he said cautiously.

"You're alive, then."

"Barely," he muttered, then added, "What's up?"

She didn't answer immediately. There was a softness to her silence this time. Not the usual barbed guilt-trip pause, but something more... tentative.

"I just... I thought maybe you could come round. For a cup of tea. Or something."

Jonah squinted into the middle distance, as if the request itself might be visible on the horizon.

"Is everything okay?"

"I don't know. I just feel... off. It's probably nothing. Forget I called."

He hesitated.

"No. I'll come."

"You will?"

"Yeah. I'll head over this afternoon."

"Alright. Don't make a mess."

She hung up before he could reply.

The words lodged under his ribs like a splinter. *Don't make a mess.* She probably meant *don't be late,* but the old sting of judgment was still there, sharp as ever. For a heartbeat he was twelve again, shrinking under the weight of her disapproval, already rehearsing apologies.

His chest tightened, fingers curling into fists on his knees. He could almost feel the tug-of-war inside him - the boy who wanted to disappear, and the man who had begun to choose something else. He shut his eyes, breathing slow, until the noise of both voices softened.

When he opened them, the world looked steady again. He unclenched his fists and smoothed the crumpled edge of his jeans, grounding himself in the present.

Something about the call left a strange taste in his mouth; not worry, not fear, but a visceral pull. Like something unfinished was waiting in the corners of that old house.

He glanced at the journal beside him in his satchel then zipped it shut with deliberate finality, as if sealing in a promise to himself. He stood, rolled his shoulders back, and let the tension drain through his heels into the earth.

It was time to go back.
But only to move forward.

....

The house was smaller than he remembered.

Or maybe Jonah had just outgrown the fear.

But as he stood in front of the gate, fingers hovering near the latch, the childhood dread settled in like a tight shirt that still somehow fit.

The lawn hadn't been mowed in weeks. The windows were yellowed with grime. A bent plastic flamingo still stood by the steps like a sentinel who'd seen too much and said nothing.

He pushed the gate open.

It squealed. Of course it did.

Inside, the air was thick with cigarette smoke and unresolved decades. A curling trail of ash floated lazily toward the ceiling, where a stained lampshade did nothing to filter the dimness.

His mother sat in her usual chair - slouched, arms crossed, ashtray balanced on one knee like a war medal.

"You came," she said flatly, exhaling a plume of smoke without meeting his eyes.

"Yeah. You called."

"Don't sound so surprised. A mother's allowed to see her only son."

Jonah stepped inside, letting the door fall shut behind him like a vault door sealing him into memory.

Elaine Vale had been beautiful once. The kind that turned heads. That beauty had hardened into bitterness. She had a voice like sandpaper and eyes that never quite looked you in the face. She looked at him sideways.

"You've lost weight," she said. "You still doing that...office thing?"

"Yeah, Mum." He lied.

"Still not married?"

"No, Mum."

"Tea's on the counter. Make it yourself if you want."

"Of course."

He moved through the kitchen, where nothing had changed. The same cracked tile. The same rusted tap. The same lingering sense that if you listened closely enough, you could hear the echoes of old arguments embedded in the walls.

He poured water into the kettle. As it boiled, he drifted.

His father shouting, words indistinct but full of venom.

His mother crying, not out of pain - but rage.

Jonah, maybe seven, maybe younger, hiding beneath the bed, his small hand reaching up to touch the underside of her mattress. Just to feel that someone was above him. That he wasn't entirely alone.

He would lie there for hours. Listening. Breathing shallow. Pressing his fingertips into the fabric above him like it could anchor him to a world that always seemed like it might drift away. Abandonment…the paralysing fear prickled his skin like a rash.

"You can't fill his head with this madness!"
"He deserves the truth! You're the one who's blind!"
"You're sick, and I won't let you ruin him too."

Then came the slam of the door.

And silence that never ended. His worst fear realised.

The kettle shrieked.

Jonah flinched.

He poured the tea, returned to the living room, and set one mug gently on the table near her ashtray. She didn't thank him. She never did.

"So?" he asked.

She looked at him then - really looked. Something in her face had shifted. A flicker of something like fear, poorly disguised as annoyance.

"There's been… something. I don't know. Strange phone calls. Letters shoved through the slot without a stamp. Just symbols. Spiral things."

Jonah froze. A cold pressure clamped the back of his neck.

"Spirals?"

She reached behind the lamp and pulled out a folded piece of paper. It looked slightly yellowed, old, hand-drawn; almost as if it had been torn from somebody's notebook. Or journal.

It was a spiral. Identical to the one on his journal, or Lucien's card. Almost identical. His eyes lingered on the linework - something about the way it curved in on itself made him feel watched.

His stomach turned.

"Where did this come from?"

"I told you. It was just here. No return address. Just slid under the door. And then the phone rang, and when I picked up, it was just… static. But I could swear someone was on the line. Breathing."

Her voice wavered. A tremor beneath the habitual sharpness. For a moment, Jonah thought he saw something close to vulnerability. Or maybe loneliness.

She stared at him, eyes narrowed. "You know something about this, don't you?"

Jonah's voice was hoarse. "No. I mean… maybe. I don't know."

"Don't lie to me, Jonah. You're your father's son."

There it was. She said it like an accusation. Like a curse.

"He used to draw things like this. Said they came to him in dreams. Said we were living in a cage made of light. That the world was a simulation built by something else. He was unwell, Jonah. And I will not watch you go down the same road."

Jonah stood up. He couldn't sit anymore. The air felt poisoned.

"Maybe he wasn't wrong," he said, staring down at the spiral in her hand. "Maybe he just saw it before anyone else."

"He left," she snapped. "He abandoned you. That's what people like him do. Float off into their fantasies while the rest of us have to clean up the mess."

He didn't respond, because she wasn't wrong. And that made it all worse.

She tossed the paper onto the coffee table. It spun slightly, settling next to the mug like an omen.

They sat, mostly in silence, with her describing the details of her increasingly fractured life - how the house creaked at night, how the shadows seemed to move, how she sometimes thought she heard whispers in the walls. And he listened, like an obedient son should, but seeing her more clearly now. How the sharpness in her tone was thin armour. How the resentment that had shaped his life had always been tangled with her own fear.

She stubbed another cigarette out. "Can you just… check the windows before you go? I keep thinking someone's watching."

He nodded, moving toward the hallway, the journal still in his satchel pressing against his side like a heartbeat.

In the back bedroom his old one - he found another spiral etched in chalk on the window. He traced it with his finger, it was on the inside. His pulse thudded.

The line was faint, half-erased by time and dust. He wiped it clean with his sleeve, fighting the rising nausea. The thought clawed at him: *This has been here for years.*

But his mind leapt elsewhere. There was only one person he associated the symbols with: Lucien.

Lucien's words replayed in his mind - *You're not broken. You're remembering.*

88

Remembering what? His mother had said his father used to draw these things too. He was suddenly confused, split open, and an icy thought crept up his spine, unbidden: *What if Lucien's not the saviour? What if he's the warden?*

What if it was a warning? *Stay asleep. Stay afraid.*

The spiral on the glass seemed to tighten the longer he looked at it, turning inward, collapsing on itself. Or maybe it was his own vision folding under the weight of doubt.

What did it mean?

His mother didn't say goodbye as he left. She never did.

Back on the pavement, the sun felt too bright. Too intentional.
He felt shaken. More than shaken - split, as though the ground itself had tilted.

He needed air.
He needed something real.

….

The train ride back into the city felt like a return to someone else's life. Jonah sat by the window, his reflection a pale ghost pressed against the dark. City lights flickered across his face like static from a dying signal.

He had walked into his mother's house feeling clear, grounded. Now everything felt brittle, and a familiar confusion crept up on him like an unwanted guest. He hadn't eaten since the tea at his mother's - he didn't care - but it added to the hollow weight he carried. The hypnotic blur of the city through the window turned his thoughts inward.

Lucien's spiral had been scratched into the window of his childhood home. The place where his fear had first taken root. The same spiral he'd thought was a symbol of awakening. Of hope. Now, it felt like a mark. A claim.

He thought about Lucien again, and frowned. Had Lucien known? Had he been watching Jonah even then? The thought made his skin itch.

Yet beneath the unease there was something stranger - when he traced that chalk spiral with his finger, he had felt a faint pull of recognition. Not toward Lucien, but toward himself. Like an echo he couldn't place, a child's scrawl long buried under dust. The idea unsettled him even more.

He scrolled through his thoughts like old photos - trying to remember why he had trusted Lucien in the first place. He had felt seen. Heard. But maybe that's what predators do best - mirror what you most need to hear.

You're not broken.
You're remembering.
You're one of us.

Now it all felt cheap. Scripted. Simulated.

And in his gut, the old ache had returned.

He thought about Sadie.
He thought about his job.
About the money he wasn't making. The sleep he wasn't having. The silence he had inherited.

His fingers buzzed with the itch of escape. Again. Maybe it was him. Perhaps his idea that the world was tilting was just an excuse for his own unresolved issues. A feeling of heaviness formed deep in his gut; like he'd swallowed a boulder that he couldn't digest. Had he been too quick to find a solution outside of himself? It was true, he'd leapt at the first thing that felt like relief.

What if none of it meant anything? What if I'm just a burnout with delusions of grandeur? What if I left everything - for nothing?

Confusion suffocated him again, wrapping tighter with each stop the train rattled past. He thought about his mother, sat all alone in her own squalor. He thought about his apartment. Was this where he was headed, and he couldn't stop it?

The panic rose in him like water filling a sealed room - slow, steady, unstoppable. He'd thought he had started to fly. Now he realised he'd just been falling all along.

He suddenly felt like a drink. He hadn't had one since he'd left work, but now the urge came back sharp, like a familiar escape hatch.

He got off at the next stop and headed straight for the bar.

The Bar

It was dim, tucked down a side alley like a secret only the broken knew about. The music pulsed low and warm - noncommittal jazz with electronic undertones. The kind of place where no one asked questions.

Jonah took a stool near the far end, nodding at the bartender.

"Whiskey," he said. "Neat." He wanted something shocking to his system. Something that would match the feeling coursing through his body. At least it may draw the attention away from the familiar ache that had started to throb again.

He downed the first like water. The second slower.

The burn didn't help.

His head dropped into his hands, elbows on the bar.

What am I even doing here?

You're running.

The voice was his own. Sharp. Honest. Inevitable.

He took his drink and made his way up to the roof terrace. It was empty and the sky was bruising into dusk, the odd star coming out, like the heavens were curious to watch what he did next. He needed air. Space. Anything that didn't smell like mildew and memories. The city hummed below like an old machine chewing its own wires.

He lit a cigarette - an old habit resurrected for no one but himself - and leaned against the iron railing, trying to forget the look in his mother's eyes. Not anger. Not bitterness. Fear. And worse, the symbol scratched into the grime of the bedroom window.

He'd wiped it away without thinking, but it had already etched itself into him.

Lucien. Could it be him?

A gust of wind cut through the rooftop and Jonah looked up.

She was there.

Not near him - across the space, silhouetted by a string of hanging bulbs that swung lazily above her like sleepy planets. Her back was to him. She hadn't seen him. But he saw her.

She stood barefoot on the concrete, looking up at the darkening sky. Jonah was captivated by her presence at once; something about her silhouette, her posture, something familiar and hypnotic that pulled deep inside his gut. As she stood, the breeze carried a small feather across her vision, and she caught it with gentle grace.

She tilted her head upward, eyes closed. Then, with impossible stillness, she raised the feather to her lips - and blew.

It should have floated a few feet before falling. Instead, the feather stopped midair.

Hung there. Suspended. Rotating slowly as if caught in the gravity of an unseen planet.

Then, as Jonah blinked, it burned - a slow, golden ember eating away at the soft white vanes, curling them into smoke that drifted upward not in plumes, but in symbols.

The same ones from the window. The same ones from the journal.

Jonah's mouth went dry.

A man emerged into the space carrying two cocktails. He was tall, dark-skinned, lean. There was something wolfish in the way he carried himself. Not threatening, just wild and unapologetic. It was if he'd waited until the performance concluded. The smoke dissipated, the lights flickered once, and the rooftop was just a rooftop again. He took a step towards the mysterious woman.

She opened her eyes and took the cocktail and they both laughed easily, casually, like he'd told a secret joke.

Then she turned and her eyes locked onto Jonah's.

And in that instant, something *split* inside him.

Not a fracture.
A remembering.

Her expression didn't change. But she tilted her head ever so slightly. As if she recognized him. As if they'd never not known each other.

Jonah crushed the cigarette into the railing, unaware that it had burned down to the filter. And watched her approach. The man, trailed behind her like a satellite - gravitationally bound, but peripheral.

She moved like wind across water. Long, messy curls. A long coat that looked like it had seen storms in cities Jonah couldn't name. Tattoos curled out from under her sleeves and across her collarbone like maps of forgotten places. She wasn't trying to be seen. She simply *was*, and the space bent to accommodate it.

She stopped directly in front of Jonah. "You look like a man who's trying to outrun himself," she says.

Jonah blinked. "Maybe I am."

"It never works."

She sat on the stool beside him. The man she was with settled on her other side, watching with idle curiosity.

"That's a waste," she said. "You've got the fire under your skin. I can smell it from here. What's your name?"

"Jonah."

"Of course it is." She tilted her head, studying him like a puzzle with missing pieces. "You don't remember me, do you?"

He blinked. "Should I?"

She didn't answer. Instead, she took his hand and turned it over - her fingers cold and electric. She traced a circle on his palm.

"You dream about symbols, don't you?" She nodded with quiet amusement to the place where she'd burnt the feather. As if she'd known that he was watching all along. "Circular ones. Spirals. Snakes eating themselves. Stars that collapse inward."

Jonah froze.

"How do you know that?"

She shrugged. "Because I've been in your dreams. Or maybe you've been in mine. It's hard to tell anymore."

She picked up her cocktail from the high table and took a sip, studying him over the rim. "Let me guess. You just saw something you can't explain. Maybe in a reflection. Or on a window. Something you're afraid means you're crazy."

Jonah blinked.

"I'm Ezra," she said, without extending her hand. "And this is Kale." Kale nodded at Jonah with a relaxed amusement like this happened to him all the time.

Ezra grinned. "You're wondering if I'm another glitch. Or a recruiter from some secret cult." That made Jonah, hold his breath. "Or maybe just very high."

His eyes narrowed slightly. "Which is it?"

"Wouldn't you like to know."

He laughed, nervously. "Right. And I suppose you know what's happening to me?"

"No," she said. "You do. You're just pretending not to. Because it's safer."

That hit harder than he expected.

She placed her drink again and leaned her elbows on the table, close now - like they were conspirators.

"You've been drifting," she said. "Job to job. Idea to idea. Searching for something, and hating yourself for not knowing what."

Jonah's breath caught again.

She went on, voice softer now. "You feel like a fraud. Like you're faking every step of being an adult. Because everyone else seems to have bought the lie and made peace with it, and you - didn't. Couldn't."

He was silent.

"You keep thinking it's you," she said. "It's not. The game is rigged. You're just one of the few who noticed the walls are made of smoke."

Jonah laughed - short, bitter. "And what? You're here to save me?"

Ezra smiled sidelong at him, eyes like something older than planets. "No. I'm just here to ask the right question."

"What's the question?"

She paused and lifted her drink from the table again. She finished it in one movement and set it down with a clink.

"Do you want to get out of your head?"

He didn't answer.

She tilted her head, curls spilling over her shoulder. "C'mon. You've done enough brooding for one apocalypse."

Then she turned and walked toward the stairwell. Kale downed his drink and pushed off the table to follow her.

Ezra glanced back. "Coming, Jonah?"

He hesitated.

Then nodded.

Ezra laughed.

"Come on, then."

The Night of Fire

Her apartment was carved out of the top floor of a converted warehouse. High ceilings. Exposed brick. Art that looked like it had been painted during storms. There were plants climbing the corners and wrapping around beams in the ceiling, which gave way to a huge skylight providing a window to the heavens that wheeled above them.

Kale moved through the space like he belonged there. He poured drinks, rolled a joint and took up space without domination.

Jonah hovered in the doorway like an apology.

"You okay?" Ezra asked, slipping off her coat, revealing more tattoos, more stories.

"I don't know," Jonah said.

"Good," she said. "Honest answer."

She handed him a drink.

"To forgetting?" he said.

"No," Ezra said. "To *uncovering*. Forgetting's what got you here."

He stepped a little further into the room which was warm and low-lit, wrapped in the scent of incense and something sweet - maybe sandalwood, maybe something

101

older. The walls bore no allegiance to logic. Tapestries draped the spaces between the climbing plants like the canopy of an unseen forest, and symbols traced in ash or paint marked doorframes and shelves. The whole place felt alive, like a living journal she had written in motion and breath.

Jonah took a few more steps in, half-certain he shouldn't be there, half-certain he'd never belonged anywhere else. Kale dropped onto one end of the long, deep sofa as if it were a throne he'd once ruled from. Jonah followed suit with less certainty, perching near the middle, hands lightly clasped around his drink as if trying not to touch anything too sacred.

And then there was Ezra.

She moved like she didn't walk - like her feet touched the earth out of affection, not gravity. Something feline threaded through her movements: ease, sensuality, precision. When she crossed the room, Jonah noticed the way her bare feet whispered against the wooden floor, how her hips knew music even when none played. She was dressed in fabric that clung in places and flowed in others, as if every thread had been summoned by her body rather than stitched for it.

She settled on the rug before them, sitting lightly, cross-legged, as though the ground itself had called her to rest. Her eyes scanned both men - dark, star-strewn, half amusement, half x-ray. She was completely comfortable in her skin. No mask. No performance. Just essence.

From somewhere beside her, she pulled the joint that Kale had rolled, and lit it with a casual flick. She inhaled, slow and reverent, then stood in a single motion so graceful it made Jonah's heart stutter. She held the joint out to him, her fingers long and open like an invitation.

He reached for it, their fingertips brushing - a spark, like static charged by something far older than either of them. The scent of her skin hit him in the same moment. Salt, earth, mystery. Jonah brought the joint to his lips, and the smoke curled through him like a memory he hadn't yet lived.

Then, Ezra turned and tossed a small remote to Kale. He caught it instinctively, grinning, and pointed it toward the corner of the room.

Music filled the space. Slow. Heavy. Laced with a velvet bass line that seemed to pulse from beneath the floorboards. It vibrated in Jonah's chest, low and primal.

And then she danced.

Right there in front of them. No announcement. No invitation. Just Ezra, barefoot and unburdened, her hair wild, her eyes like constellations. At first, just movement. Like smoke had decided to take human form. Her body moved with zero self-consciousness - pure embodiment, no pretence. Her hair flowed, tumbling like roots down her back. Her hands didn't follow the beat; they summoned it. She was like a high priestess of some ancient rite, moving like she was underwater, and her body - lightning wrapped in silk - unfurled rhythm in every breath. She didn't dance for them, exactly. She danced because something inside her needed to be remembered.

But still - Jonah couldn't look away.

Kale leaned forward, equally transfixed, as if some tether inside him had been pulled taut. Jonah felt it too - that low, rising echo of something ancestral. As if Ezra's feminine had reached out, not to seduce, but to awaken. To coax the masculine from sleep and demand its witnessing.

Jonah took another drag. The smoke spiralled up as she moved. And for the first time in longer than he could remember, he felt something deeper than curiosity. He felt... pulled. Called. Like part of him had been waiting for this frequency, and now it had found him.

He exhaled slowly; eyes locked on the woman dancing in front of him.

Ezra. An invocation wrapped in skin. A cipher he hadn't yet learned how to read.

But God - he wanted to.

Then, she turned.

And the universe stopped.

Ezra looked directly at Jonah like she already knew who he was. Not the outer him - the exhausted, performative husk - but the part beneath. The part even he couldn't look at for long. Her gaze was surgical and sacred all at once.

She smiled - not warmly, but with amusement. Like she was remembering a joke from a past life.

"You look like you lost something," she said, her voice low and earthy. "Or maybe like you just found it and are terrified."

Jonah laughed, awkwardly. He'd forgotten how to speak, but found the words. "Bit of both."

She took a step closer, and her presence was animal. It was as if Gaia herself had taken human form; just to see how it felt to take a body and experience the world through senses for the first time. Raw. A lioness who'd read too many gospels and burned them all.

She lifted her top over her head and threw it on the floor where it nestled in a coil of silk and scent. Her breasts, her stomach, her ribs were all covered in tattoos and Jonah's breath caught. Spirals, glyphs…things he'd seen in his dreams, his journal. Exactly. An eye inside a descending triangle, inked in black and red, keys with missing teeth … a spiral with an opening eye in the centre.

He gasped. "You…"

Her mouth pressed to his ear. "Shhh," she whispered. "Don't make it conscious yet. That kills the magic."

She lifted herself and pushed a breast towards his mouth; the nipple quivered through ink and heat. His mouth opened and he spiralled - the alcohol, the joint were nothing compared to the intoxication from the energy she exuded like a small sun. She whispered as he sucked, and she writhed on his body… "This isn't about sex… this is about rebirth." Her words were like a gently pulsing mantra, disarming, drawing him deeper. "This isn't about the body…this is about waking up."

The air was thick with permission, and he felt Kale move next to him, his hand on his thigh. Not threatening, just *open*. Jonah didn't pull away. He kissed his shoulder and moved to the back of his neck. A low, primal moan, deep from somewhere in his distant past, rattled in his throat like a vibration from a life he'd long forgotten.

Jonah didn't know how his clothes came off or how their bodies found rhythm. It didn't matter. What mattered was how Ezra *looked at him* - not with hunger, but with *recognition*. Like every touch was reactivating an ancient frequency.

In amongst the chaos of skin and breath he suddenly saw what wasn't clear before: "The body remembers what the mind denies."

They moved like elements.

No power games. No ego.

Just breath, sweat, release.

Jonah let go in their arms, shed shame like old skin, let the last of the noise be burned in touch.

And when he finally collapsed back onto the cushions, tangled between them both, eyes blinking up at the skylight that showed only stars, Ezra leaned into his ear and whispered:

"You were never broken, Jonah. You were just waiting for someone who saw through the glass."

He didn't respond.

But his heart did.

There, lay on his back, entwined, looking up at stars, a single tear released from his opening eye and the ache inside him quieted.

Embers in the Wake

The morning light poured into Ezra's apartment like a silent hymn.

Jonah stirred beneath a loose tangle of limbs, half-draped across a sun-stained sheet. Kale was already gone - vanished like mist with the sunrise - but Ezra lay beside him, still, breathing deep. Wild even in sleep. Untamed.

He traced a curl of hair that had fallen across her cheek, then slipped quietly out from under the covers. He dressed without noise. One last glance at the feathered earring lying on the nightstand - a small token of chaos and remembrance - and then he left.

Outside, the city felt *new*. Not cleaner or quieter, just… more dimensional. Like layers had shifted in the night. The traffic didn't seem so random. The movement of people felt choreographed, but not entirely by them. Jonah walked through it like a ghost slowly regaining density.

By the time he reached his apartment building, his mind was already caught between wonder and doubt.

Graham was watering the dead succulents near the lobby.

"Well look what the cat finally dragged in," Graham called as Jonah pushed the door open. "You've had people looking for you, kid. Your work rang. Some weird guy in a green coat too. Said he was an old friend."

Jonah paused. "Lucien?"

"Didn't give a name. Just one of those voices, you know? All smooth, no meaning."

Jonah forced a half-smile. "Thanks, Graham."

"Jonah," Graham said, lowering his voice. "Whatever you're caught up in… just keep your feet on the ground, alright? You've always been a good kid. Don't get blown away."

Jonah nodded, swallowing something tight in his throat.

"I'll try."

The Banana Buddha was sat on his doorstep, still with traces of rubber plant soil behind its Ray Bans. A message from Elliot, retrieved from the plant pot but now sat silently on the cold tiled floor; its plastic gaze no longer smug, just sad. He scooped it up on the way through the door.

The apartment was still a mess.

The takeout container from his last real meal had begun to ferment into science.

Jonah stripped off his clothes, stood under the shower until the steam wiped his thoughts clean, then dressed in something neutral. Grounding. A grey t-shirt. Black jeans. He looked in the mirror, half-expecting not to see himself.

But he was still there.
Just… deeper. Sharper.

He opened the journal.
And blinked.

New words.

"*You found the flame. But fire does not stay still. She moves, Jonah. She burns.*"

The handwriting was his, but not. The letters curved like his own hand might shape them, but there was a weight, an age, a gravity that wasn't his. Almost as if an echo of someone else's touch pressed through him.

His chest tightened. A voice, half-forgotten, stirred inside the lines. A resonance. Like memory disguised as ink.

But the words shimmered faintly too, as though resisting the page - unstable, alive, reluctant to be fixed. And in that shimmer he caught the uncanny sense that it was a part of him he hadn't yet grown into.

She…

He knew who it meant.
Ezra.

But what did it mean?
Was she his saviour?
His next test?
His mirror?

She burns…

His heart pounded - not with fear, but with urgency. Something had begun. Something more than him, older than him, written from a place he could not yet reach.

And he wasn't ready to name it.
Not yet.
But it had lit a fuse.

He picked up the journal, zipped it into his bag, and laced his boots with deliberate movements. His fingers didn't tremble this time.

He glanced around the apartment once before he left. It didn't feel like home anymore.

Then he stepped out into the light.
And walked straight toward Lucien.

Velvet Chains

The coffee shop was too bright. That morning clarity that cuts through illusions. Jonah stepped inside, half-hoping Lucien wouldn't be there - half certain he would.

He spotted him in the corner by the window, already seated, a cup of something herbal steaming in his hand. Lucien looked immaculate, as always: pale blue shirt, collar open just enough to suggest ease, not effort. He looked like serenity carved from stone.

Jonah, on the other hand, had barely slept. But something about him had shifted. Even behind the shadows under his eyes, he carried a new vitality. The residue of the night with Ezra clung to him like ozone after a storm.

Lucien noticed immediately.

"You look well," he said, as Jonah sat down. "Clearer. Something's lifted."

Jonah tried not to smile. "I slept. For once." He lied.

Lucien studied him. "Or perhaps... you remembered something."

Jonah didn't reply. The waitress came. He ordered a black coffee, then looked back at Lucien.

"I went to see my mother yesterday."

Lucien raised his eyebrows, just slightly. "Brave man."

"She seemed... nervous. Unsettled."

Lucien's face didn't flicker.

Jonah studied him. "There were symbols on the window in my old room. Hand-drawn."

"Really?" Lucien leaned in slightly. "What kind of symbols?"

Jonah shrugged. "Similar to the ones I've seen before. Journal-type symbols."

Lucien's expression was a perfect blend of curiosity and concern - nothing out of place. But Jonah felt something ripple behind it. A flicker too practiced.

He pressed further. "You don't know anything about that?"

Lucien tilted his head. "I know symbols show up when someone is close to remembering. Sometimes that proximity spreads to others. It's not uncommon. Energy leaves a residue."

Jonah nodded slowly, pretending to accept it. But inside, the uncertainty pulsed.

Lucien sipped his tea, then set it down with intention. "Actually... since we're sharing secrets."

Jonah raised an eyebrow.

Lucien leaned forward, voice dropping just slightly. "I was the one who left the journal."

The words landed like a slow fuse. Jonah blinked. "You... what?"

"I left it on your doorstep. Thought you'd find it when you were ready."

"But you told me nothing about it."

Lucien smiled gently. "Would you have opened it if I had?"

Jonah opened his mouth. Closed it. He didn't know the answer.

Lucien continued, "It was just a seed, Jonah. Something to nudge you awake. And it worked, didn't it? And now look at you. Clear-eyed. Centred. There's power in you again."

Jonah looked down at his coffee, brow furrowed. Everything in him wanted to draw a line - to make sense of who Lucien was. But the edges kept blurring.

Lucien leaned back, exuding warmth now, paternal almost.

"I know you're torn," he said. "And that's good. Healthy. But the path isn't always light or dark. Sometimes it's both. Sometimes the devil wears linen and the saviour shows up barefoot."

Jonah glanced up sharply.

Lucien smiled again. "You'll know more after the retreat. You're already booked, after all."

"That was before…" Jonah hesitated.

"Before?" Lucien tilted his head, curious.

His voice was quieter. "I met someone."

Lucien paused.

"Oh?"

"Her name's Ezra."

Lucien didn't blink.

But something… shifted.

The warmth remained. But it became a contained warmth. Like light behind a locked door.

"And what does she do?"

"She asks questions. Tells the truth. Makes me feel like I'm not going crazy."

Lucien's smile stayed. But the stillness underneath it sharpened.

"Be careful with people like that."

"Like what?"

"False prophets," Lucien said gently. "They burn bright. They offer rebellion wrapped in seduction. But they serve themselves more than truth."

Jonah bristled. "You don't know her."

"I know the type," Lucien replied, folding his hands. "Unstable. Addicted to chaos. Drawn to the newly awakened because they're easy to imprint on."

Jonah narrowed his eyes.

Lucien leaned back, the performance returning.

"But I'm not here to make enemies. I'm here to invite you forward. You've come so far, Jonah. But there's still more.

Jonah didn't answer.

Lucien's smile softened, almost sad. "You'll be among like-minded people. People who've stepped outside the pattern, like you. You'll get clarity there."

He stood, smoothing his shirt as if brushing off invisible dust. "And who knows - by the end of it, you'll know whether I'm your devil or your guide."

He reached out, placing a hand lightly on Jonah's shoulder.

"Either way, I'll see you there."

Then he turned, moving through the café like he belonged in every room he entered.

Jonah watched him go, the words echoing: *I left the journal.*

Part of him wanted to believe it. That Lucien had seen his potential, believed in him, guided him here.

Another part couldn't ignore the cold flicker behind his eyes.

Ezra had warned him. Lucien had smiled.

And now the choice was his.

The Shape of the Cage

The café was on a quiet side street where the city forgot to be loud.

No signs. No music. Just chipped white metal chairs, climbing ivy, and light filtered through the kind of trees that shouldn't survive in this part of town. It felt like a place in between things - a pocket of reality someone had accidentally left unguarded.

Jonah arrived early. He hated that he did.

He felt slightly awkward texting her, but then excited by how fast she'd replied. And now he sat with a black coffee that had long gone cold, heart buzzing like static.

And then…

She arrived.

Ezra stepped through the archway with the sun behind her, haloing her like a force of nature wearing a flowing skirt that clung to her like the wind had followed her in. Her hair was wild again, wind-tousled and unapologetic. A single feather earring dangled from her left ear, shifting with her steps like it had its own rhythm.

She was alone.

And for a flicker of a moment, Jonah forgot how to breathe.

"Hey," he said, standing instinctively.

"Hey yourself," she replied, sliding into the chair across from him like they'd done this a hundred times before.

"You look like you've been dropped from a great height," she said pouring herself a water.

"Maybe I have," Jonah murmured. "I haven't decided if I landed or not."

She didn't fidget. Didn't sip. Just stared at him - seeing him in that way that made Jonah either want to run or confess everything.

"You look different," she said.

"I feel different."

A pause.

"Kale not with you today?" he asked, trying to sound casual.

Ezra barked a laugh, full of wild warmth.

"You think he's mine?"

Jonah shrugged. "You seemed... close."

"I'm close with a lot of things. Stars. Oceans. Death." She smirked. "But no one owns me, Jonah. I'm not furniture. I move."

That should've made him more cautious.

Instead, it made him feel *alive*.

"You're intense," he said, and she grinned wider.

"And you're still waking up."

They both laughed.

She looked up and smiled at a waiter. He was hovering like he'd been waiting for a sign from her. She was impossible to miss in a room, and right now, it felt like the whole universe was listening and watching. She ordered a coffee, and he scurried off like he'd been given a secret by an alchemist.

Jonah sat back in his chair and looked at her. Really looked. "I'm not sure I understand all this, what's going on, or…who you are?"

She sipped her water and leaned forward slightly, elbows on the table. "I'm someone who unplugged. Someone who saw the pattern. Once you see it, you can't unsee it." She looked hard at Jonah. "Which is what has started for you."

"What is?" asked Jonah.

"The unravelling…you're starting to see through the illusion."

Jonah watched her. "I need you to tell me what's happening. I need it straight. No riddles, no metaphors."

She looked over at him, studying him for a long moment.

"Okay," she said. "You ready to have your bones unthreaded?"

"Sure," he said, exhaling. "What's a little existential dismemberment between friends." The word 'friends' seemed awkward in his mouth, it created a pull somewhere he couldn't place.

Ezra sat upright, took a breath, and in that breath, the world seemed to lean in too.

"Earth is not what you think it is. It never was. It's not just a planet. It's a node. A junction point in a multiverse of overlapping simulations."

Jonah blinked, then laughed. "Simulations."

She didn't laugh. "I'm serious. A simulation, yes - but not just a virtual construct. It's a psychic framework. An engineered system designed by intelligences far older and colder than we can imagine. We call them the Greys. Not because we know what they are… but because we *don't*."

Jonah's brow furrowed. "You're saying…aliens?"

Ezra shrugged. "Maybe. Maybe something else entirely. What matters is what they did. They seeded this place with us - biological humans. Creators. Feelers. Consciousness in raw form. But they feared what we could become."

"Why?"

"Because they lost what we still carry," she said, tapping her chest. "Source. Love. Creative essence. They became advanced - but severed. Technologically superior, but spiritually extinct."

She paused, letting that sink in.

"So they did what you do when you want to control a dangerous species. You clip its wings."

"How?"

"DNA," she said simply. "We were designed to carry twelve strands - twelve frequencies of perception. But they cut ten. What's left?" She raised two fingers. "Survival. Binary thought. Linear time. Just enough to build, breed, obey, and die."

Jonah felt a chill crawl over his skin. He sat back, as if the idea physically pressed against him. His pulse in his ears now.

Ezra continued, her voice low but vibrating.

"And to keep us playing their game, they installed The Veil."

"Which is?"

"A suppression system. A living network of forgetfulness. Not one thing - *everything*. It's layered across every system you were raised in" Ezra went on. "A *network*. A saturation of ideas, beliefs and agreements designed to keep you small."

She counted on her fingers:

"School? Teaches you what to think, not how.
Pharma? It dulls the gut - the compass to truth.
Bureaucracy, even in spirituality? Forms over essence.
Compliance over revelation.
Media? Fear loops and dopamine traps.
Social justice, identity wars, moral outrage? Distraction dressed as meaning."

Jonah stared. The words weren't new - but the clarity was. The simplicity of it. He thought of his dream, the model in work that he'd built unconsciously.

He swallowed. "So everything's a trap?"

"No," Ezra said. "Everything is a mirror. The Veil reflects how far you are from yourself."

Jonah thought about the dull ache he'd had all his life. The feeling that something was missing.

She leaned in.

"The purpose?" she asked. "Extraction."

He whispered, "Of what?"

"Creative energy," Ezra said. "Unlived dreams. Suppressed truths. All that untapped life force? It's the rarest currency in the multiverse. They've forgotten how to generate it, so they harvest it from us. That ache you carry?" She pointed again to his chest. "That's the signal. The dissonance between who you are… and who you were trained to be. That tension? It powers their world. The dreams you shelved. The songs you never wrote. The words you swallowed. The touch you denied. That's *fuel* to them."

Jonah thought of the cubicles, the copywriting briefs, the glassy smiles. He thought of Sadie, of Lucien, of his mother whispering about shadows she couldn't name.

He thought of the journal. The symbols. The way it had buzzed in his hands.

"I've felt this… all my life," he said.

Ezra nodded. "We all do. But most people medicate, rationalise, distract, obey. You asked instead."

Jonah stared into the middle distance. His pulse thudded behind his eyes. The words were unbelievable. *Except they weren't.*

"This is insane," he muttered.

"But it explains everything, doesn't it?" She offered gently.

He licked his lips. "The glitches… the loops…"

She nodded. "Cracks in the render. When the soul starts remembering, the code starts to break. The simulation can't hold you anymore. So it glitches. You see through."

Jonah closed his eyes.

The symbols.

The journal.

Terry's looped conversation.

It all began to rearrange inside him - *clicking*.

Ezra watched him ride the wave.

"They'll tell you it's anxiety. Fatigue. Brain fog. That you're unstable. They'll medicate the symptoms. But you're not going mad, Jonah. You're waking up."

He suddenly opened his eyes. "And Lucien?"

Ezra tilted her head slightly, curious.

"If he's what I think he is," her expression hardened a shade. Not bitter - just knowing. "He's a gatekeeper. One of many. Not evil. Just bound. His job is to keep you compliant while believing you're free. That's the real trick."

125

"He said the same about you."

Ezra smirked. "Of course he did."

"So how do I know who to trust?"

"You don't," she said simply. "That's the point."

Her voice didn't rise. She didn't lean in like a conspirator. She just said it like the weather.

"So what do I do with that?" Jonah asked. "You both can't be right."

"Maybe neither of us is," she said. "Not everybody is what they seem." There was something heavy about that sentence. Something that she wasn't saying.

"I thought he was helping me."

"He *was* - in the beginning. They always do. They give you breadcrumbs. Just enough magic to keep you on the leash. They always try to call you home when you start building wings."

The waiter brought her coffee and placed it with some reverence in front of her. He paused, as if he was waiting like the rest of the universe. She dismissed him with a smile.

Jonah blinked.

She softened.

"There's no saviour coming Jonah. Not him. Not me. Only you. This system was built to make you forget that." She took a sip of her coffee.

"I'm not your guide, Jonah. I'm not here to hand you a map. I walked through my own fire. Alone. You'll have to do the same."

She cradled the coffee cup in front of her. The feather earring swayed slightly.

"I can tell you what I've seen. What I know. But truth's not an instruction manual."

She looked at Jonah again. Direct, clean.

'Truth is, you can't really move forward unless you've removed your own blocks. You must do your own work Jonah. If you still have a little boy in there trying to please his mother…" she touched his heart gently and Jonah felt an icicle of shame stab the pit of his stomach. His mind flashed: *stupid boy. A cigarette dangling from a hard mouth.*

She waited for the moment to land "…then the Veil will exploit that need in you, giving you everything you feel you need, which is always *outside* of yourself. Maybe, if you're still looking outside of yourself, you're not ready." She said.

Jonah thought about that. Leaned in.

"And if I am?"

Ezra smiled, her voice suddenly warm again, teasing but deep.

"And if you've done the work…" she said, her tone changing to something with a little more gravity, "you see the Veil for what it is and you're ready to find who you really are."

They sat in silence for a moment, the city going about its sleepwalking business beyond the vines.

Finally, she stood.

"You're on your edge, Jonah. That's good. It's where real choices live."

She reached up and unclasped the feather earring from her left ear.

Held it out to him.

"Take it. A reminder. Not of me. Of *you*. Of the you that already knows."

Jonah took it, fingers brushing hers.

The feather was light, but it hummed with weight.

She smiled.

"You find the edge of the map. And then you burn it."

"And you?"

Ezra smirked.

"I set fires."

Then she turned and walked away.

Jonah looked at the feather in his palm, a heartbeat thundering in his chest, and the slow, seismic shift of someone about to *choose*.

The Garden of Stillness

The drive to the retreat took Jonah through endless roads flanked by unremarkable countryside. Hills rolled like indifferent shoulders beneath a grey sky, and sheep stared with the vacant serenity of creatures untroubled by awakening. His phone signal dropped an hour before he arrived, and with it, the last tether to the world he knew.

He wasn't afraid.

He was numb.

The entrance was a wrought iron gate arched with climbing roses - perfect, symmetrical, curated in a way that made them feel false, like silk flowers arranged for a funeral.

A gravel road led to the main complex: minimalist wood and stone, all open spaces and glass walls. Everything smelled like eucalyptus and something sweetly sterile - like spiritual disinfectant.

Lucien stood at the threshold; arms open like a father welcoming a prodigal son.

"Jonah," he said, the corners of his eyes crinkling. "You've arrived. This is the first step back to yourself."

They embraced. Jonah noticed that Lucien's hug was firm, too long, and when he stepped back, his hands lingered on Jonah's shoulders - anchoring him.

"You'll feel disoriented at first," Lucien said, leading him through the main hall. "That's the trauma of separation loosening its grip."

Jonah nodded, trying to shake the odd chill in his chest.

Inside, there were others. Maybe twenty in total - diverse, quiet, luminous in that curated Instagram way. Everyone seemed to move slower than natural, their smiles gentle, their eyes glazed.

"Here, we empty the mind," Lucien explained as they passed a stone basin of still water. "And in the emptiness, the soul remembers its place."

Jonah glanced at the water. His reflection didn't ripple.

Rooms were small but immaculate. One bed. One white robe. One wooden bowl with a handwritten note:

"No past. No future. Only the breath."

Jonah sighed and dropped his bag. He tried the window, but it didn't open.

. . . .

That night, the ceremony began. The room was circular, candlelit, and smelled of sage and rosewater. Lucien stood in the centre, flanked by two women dressed in flowing white, eyes closed, hands in mudras.

"Tonight," Lucien said, "we strip the noise. We release our names, our stories, our burdens. Here, there is no ego. Only essence."

Everyone was instructed to chant. Jonah joined in, reluctantly at first, then with a strange compulsion. The sound buzzed through him, making his chest vibrate, but it wasn't freeing. It felt... programmed.

When he closed his eyes, he saw not light, but static.

After the ceremony, Jonah wandered the moonlit gardens. The stars were unusually bright - too bright, like a simulation trying too hard to be real.

He sat on a bench beneath a silver-leafed tree and pulled Ezra's feather from his pocket. Ran it between his fingers like a worry stone.

"You feel it, don't you?" came a voice from the shadows.

Jonah turned. A young man stood there. Pale, twitchy, eyes darting like birds.

"Feel what?" Jonah asked.

"The dissonance. The too-perfect peace. I've been here three times. Every time, I come back emptier."

"Why do you keep coming back?"

"Because I'm afraid," the man whispered. "They told me I wouldn't make it without them."

Jonah's breath caught.

That night, he didn't sleep. The walls hummed faintly, like low-frequency hypnosis. His dreams were full of eyes watching from behind mirrors.

….

In the morning, he met Lucien for tea in a garden that looked too symmetrical to be natural. Everything in rows. Everything contained.

"How do you feel?" Lucien asked.

Jonah hesitated.
"Better," he lied.

Lucien's smile thinned.
"Sometimes," he said, stirring his tea, "the ego fights truth. It manufactures resistance. You must trust the process. Surrender completely."

He sipped his tea, gaze lingering a moment too long on the steam. "You feel the resistance," he went on. "That's good. It means there's still something to offer."

"Or something worth keeping," Jonah murmured.

Lucien chuckled softly, but the sound was dry. "You mistake possession for protection. The illusion of control. True awakening comes when we step into the void."

There was a pause, and for a flicker Jonah thought he saw something behind Lucien's eyes - like a man who once stepped toward the same void and found it waiting with teeth.

Lucien set the cup down carefully. "The hardest chains to break," he said more quietly, "are the ones we forge from love, from memory. I know that." His tone tightened, and he looked away, smoothing the edge of his sleeve as if sealing the thought back inside.

He let the silence hang.

"Tonight is the final ceremony. Total surrender. Everyone brings something that anchors them to the past. A wound, a comfort, a lie. They place it in the fire. And they rise."

Jonah stared at the water. The reflection of the trees rippled like oil.

"I don't know what to bring," he said.

Lucien tilted his head.
"You will."

Jonah nodded again, but something cracked in him. It was small. But it was there.

The Fire Offering

The air was thick with sandalwood and the pulse of low drums. The circle had been drawn in salt and ash, surrounding a large copper basin filled with dry wood and an unnatural, glowing ember that never seemed to fade.

Tonight was the Ceremony of Surrender.

Lucien stood at the centre, robes flowing, a polished smile barely veiling something sharp behind his eyes.

"Tonight," he began, "we sever ties to the illusions that hold us. We offer what no longer serves our awakening. We burn the veils of identity, and rise reborn in our true frequency."

One by one, the participants approached the fire.

A woman dropped in a photograph.

A man burned his wedding ring.

Another, a passport.

Each act followed by chants, applause, and gentle tears. Each object a brick in the prison they'd constructed around themselves. Jonah watched with a cocktail of awe and unease. Something felt hollow beneath the devotion. Like performance without pulse.

When it was his turn, he stood slowly, every bone vibrating. His robe felt tight around his throat. He walked to the basin.

Lucien greeted him with a soft nod. There was expectation in his eyes. And challenge.

"And what will you offer?" he asked.

Jonah looked down at his hands. They were trembling. He'd brought nothing - at least nothing he was prepared to burn.

And then Lucien's voice came again, lower this time, silken, in that intimate way he used when he wanted to bypass thought.

"How about the feather? You've been holding onto it like a talisman. But it's a tether, isn't it? To the self that resists surrender."

The circle was silent.

All eyes turned.

The feather.

Ezra's feather.

Jonah's fingers clutched it unconsciously at the edge of his robe, as he had each night since receiving it. It was smooth and curved, striped in copper and obsidian, almost unreal in how it shimmered.

It linked him to that night, to a different kind of ache.

He stepped toward the fire.

Lucien's smile widened.

"Release it, Jonah. Become free."

Jonah stood over the flame. He raised the feather slightly, feeling the heat licking at his fingers.

A vision struck him - Ezra's eyes staring through him in the night, wild and unwavering. Her voice:

"They'll ask you to forget. But forgetting is death in slow motion."

His heart thundered.

"Burn it," Lucien said, with a softness so sharp it cut.

And something in Jonah broke - not in submission, but in refusal. The fracture was clean, necessary.

He lowered the feather.

Then stepped back.

"No," he said.

The silence was immediate and seismic.

Lucien's eyes flickered. The mask wavered.

"You resist," he said, tone tightening. "But resistance is the ego's last gasp. You'll come to see this."

"No," Jonah said again, louder this time. "This isn't surrender. It's erasure."

He turned from the fire.

Lucien's voice followed him, no longer warm.

"You're not ready."

Jonah kept walking.

"You'll crawl back."

He kept walking.

"You'll drown without us."

Still, he walked.

Out of the circle. Out of the compound. Into the cold and unfiltered night.

He didn't know where he would go.

He didn't know what would happen next.

But for the first time in weeks, maybe years, he felt real.

Dark Reflection

Lucien remained at the fire long after the others had dispersed. The embers glowed like a constellation trying to remember its shape, each crack of wood punctuating the silence Jonah had left behind.

He sat very still, the robe heavy on his shoulders, hands folded like a man in prayer. But it wasn't prayer.

It was calculation.

Jonah's refusal replayed itself in his mind - the tremor in his hand, the flame on his skin, the word *no* splitting the air like an axe. He had seen that word before. Spoken it himself once, years ago, when he too had stood at the edge of fire.

For a moment the memory pressed hard: a younger Lucien, all raw nerve and wonder, standing before his own teacher. He had tasted the freedom Jonah now clung to. He had reached for it. And then the bargain came. The offer. The path that led him here.

Power. Ascension. A seat at the table of the architects. Not freedom - but dominion.

He had told himself it was survival. That one day, when he was strong enough, he might even turn the system inside out. But the years had sanded that promise down to something smaller. Safer. Now it was only this: keep order. Keep the rebels contained. Deliver results, and the ladder keeps extending upward. Fail, and the ladder vanishes beneath his feet.

His jaw tightened. Jonah's defiance wasn't just dangerous. It was contagious. Others might follow. And if they slipped beyond his hand, the Greys would see weakness in him. He had seen what happens when one of their servants falters. Stripped of sovereignty, devoured by the very network they once upheld.

His eyes narrowed at the fire. Jonah was not just a boy resisting initiation. He was a fracture - a living reminder of the path Lucien had turned away from.

A pulse of regret stirred in his chest, sharp and fleeting. He wondered - just for a heartbeat - what it would have been to keep walking that other road. To risk oblivion for the taste of truth. To keep the fire, instead of selling it.

Then he smothered the thought.

He leaned forward, holding his hand over the flame until the heat bit his skin. The pain steadied him.

"Not again," he murmured, voice low, meant for no one but the night. "I won't lose what I've built."

The fire popped, sending sparks into the dark like tiny rebellions. Lucien watched them vanish into the night sky.

Then he rose, smoothing his robe, his face once more composed.

If Jonah would not surrender, then he would be broken another way.

Lucien would see to it.

The Hollowing

The forest swallowed Jonah like a vague memory.

He had no direction when he left the retreat, only *motion*. His feet moved with the momentum of refusal - of Lucien, of illusion, of every story he'd inherited and outgrown. The trees thickened as he descended the unmarked slope beyond the retreat grounds, each branch reaching like a question he couldn't yet answer.

Twilight fell, and still, he walked.

Leaves stuck to his damp clothes. Sweat cooled into chills. The silence out here was feral, indifferent. The simulation's hum - ever-present in the city - was *quieter* now. Not gone. But distant. Like it couldn't follow him here. Not fully.

He collapsed near a fallen tree just before night claimed everything.

No fire. No food. No signal.

Just the sound of his breath. The dull ache in his bones. The vastness of the dark.

He lay back on the earth, fingers digging into the soil as if needing proof that something was real. That *he* was.

The sky yawned open above him. The stars - if they were stars - blinked cold and knowing.

"I've got nothing," he whispered to them.

His voice felt too loud, even if it were thin and hoarse.

"No job. No safety net. No backup plan. Nothing."

The forest did not answer.

So he closed his eyes.

And dreamed.

It wasn't a dream in the usual sense - it was a *visitation*.

He stood in a vast hall, made not of stone or wood but of *frequency*. Walls of pulsing sound. Symbols danced in the air like fireflies, familiar to the journal and the visions. But now they moved around him, through him, inviting, demanding.

A voice - not male, not female - echoed within.

"What is left when the scaffolding falls?"

He turned, and behind him were structures - images of his life: an office desk, a childhood bedroom, a framed degree, Sadie's laughter in a bar, Lucien's offered hand.

One by one, they caught fire.

Turned to smoke.

Gone.

The voice came again.

"What is yours, Jonah Vale?"

He looked down at his hands.

Empty.

And yet - they glowed.

From within.

A warmth not of ego or memory, but essence.

He wept - not in sorrow, but in recognition.

The scaffolding had never been the home. Only the shell.

The hollowing wasn't loss.

It was *permission*.

He woke just before dawn, curled against the base of an ancient tree.

The cold had soaked into him, and he shivered as the first amber rays sliced through the branches. Dew clung to his lashes. His hands were raw, dirt under his nails. A man unmade.

But in that moment, he had never felt more *true*.

There was no noise in his head.

No loop.

No ache for approval.

Just breath.

And a sense of forward.

He stood slowly, stretching joints that cracked like old floorboards.

"So that's what it takes," he muttered.

He looked up at the sky.

"Alright, then."

He turned, and with steady steps, began walking.

Toward the city.

Toward the unknown.

Toward her.

Ezra.

But this time, not as a man lost in searching.

Now, he walked with emptiness as compass.

And it pointed home.

Through the Unseen Gate

The streets blurred at the edges. Sounds stretched, collapsed. Every billboard looked like a symbol. Every repeated song on the radio felt like a coded message. He was still inside the simulation - but something had shifted. It was loosening its grip. Slipping.

He was changing.

The retreat was two days behind him. Or maybe it had been two years. Time had become elastic. All he knew was that the feather still rested in his coat pocket, and the echo of Lucien's voice still whispered when he closed his eyes:

"You'll crawl back…"

He hadn't. And he wouldn't.

Still, a pressure gathered behind his eyes - a knowing that the next step wouldn't come from thought alone. It had to come from resonance; somewhere deeper inside him.

He met Ezra near the edge of town, high up and overlooking the docks, where the water churned in black waves and the cranes stood like sleeping titans against the sodium haze. She was waiting beside a chain-link fence, a leather satchel slung across her shoulder, her boots caked in mud and ash.

She looked at him like she'd been watching from behind the sky.

"You came," she said.

"I had nowhere else to go."

She nodded once, solemn and soft.

"That's how you know you're ready."

They didn't embrace. They just *stood*, the silence between them more intimate than touch. She nodded her head, and they ducked through the fence and walked towards the trees above.

They reached the edge of the forest just as dusk began to bleed into indigo. The last light clung to the leaves like gold dust before retreating, and ahead, nestled in the undergrowth, was an old greenhouse swallowed by time and vines. To the untrained eye, it was ruin. But Jonah had learned by now that nothing was ever what it seemed.

Ezra paused at the threshold, her silhouette framed by tangled ivy and cracked glass refracting fractured moonlight.

"This is it," she said. "The perimeter. Beyond here, we're not just stepping into space - we're stepping out of ordinary perception."

Jonah's chest tightened. He looked down at his hands. They felt real. Solid. Still his. But a lingering doubt coiled at the edge of thought.

"What happens in there?" he asked.

Ezra didn't answer him, instead she reached into her satchel and pulled out a small, black object - smooth, palm-sized, like obsidian moulded into the shape of a teardrop. Faintly, it pulsed with an inner light. Not like any technology Jonah had ever seen. It hummed like a tuning fork pressed to a deeper note inside his bones.

She handed it to him.

"It's a lens," she said. "Not for your eye. For your frequency."

Jonah turned it over in his hand. "What does it do?"

Ezra hesitated.

Then, quietly: "It confirms."

His brow furrowed. "Confirms what?"

"That you're one of us," she said.

There was a pause. It fell like a stone in a still lake.

"You're testing me?" His voice cracked slightly. "Now?"

Her gaze didn't flinch. "Yes."

He stared at the lens. "You think I might be... what? One of *them*? Or...*digital*?"

148

Ezra's expression softened - not with regret, but with compassion. She stepped closer.

"Jonah… this isn't a matter of trust. It's protocol. The protections around the base are ancient, reactive, and absolute. If you'd tried to cross the threshold without being cleared…" She left the sentence unfinished, the silence more chilling than words.

He swallowed. "I thought you knew me."

"I do," she said. "But the system's deception runs deep. Even the rendered ones think they're real. They have full lives. Full memories. They dream. They cry. But they were *written*, not born."

Jonah's stomach turned. The notion clawed at the foundation of his identity. He looked down at the object in his hand, and suddenly it weighed more than stone.

"So," he said, "how many of *us* are left?"

She hesitated.

"Fewer than you think. There are more synthetic constructs now than biologicals. Most people? They're just code - reflections. Not bad, just… not *awake*. They can't hold contradiction. Can't process novelty. Can't remember."

"So how do we know who's real?"

She looked at him with a half-smile. She touched the device in his hand and lifted it, until it hovered in front of his heart.

"As well as this…you feel it. The real ones itch. They vibrate against the grain. Like splinters in the script. They feel what you felt…like there was something you'd forgotten, something that was missing."

Jonah nodded, understanding.

"I don't know if I want to know."

Ezra touched his shoulder gently. "That's the final gate, Jonah. The willingness to *see*."

He nodded, slowly, and Ezra pressed the device to his chest. It vibrated faintly, then bloomed with light - iridescent, prismed like a stained-glass window catching fire. It cast strange symbols across his skin.

Then… it dimmed.

Ezra exhaled, visibly relieved.

"You're real," she said. "Of course you are."

He looked up at her. "But you weren't sure."

"I was," she replied. "Intuitively. But intuition isn't enough anymore. Not when the Veil adapts. This… confirms what I already knew."

He gave a shaky laugh. "You could've warned me."

"I did," she said, smiling. "Just not in words."

The mood shifted subtly. The fear bled into anticipation. Ezra leaned down, touched the cracked floor of the greenhouse, and a symbol beneath the moss lit up with a soft blue glow. A low-frequency hum vibrated through the ground.

One by one, hidden doors opened - not like mechanical slides, but like ideas changing their mind. The walls bent. The air thickened. Space seemed to fold and unfold again in new geometries.

"What is this?"

"A blind spot in the simulation," she said. "The Veil can't see in. Not directly. It's one of the few places left where sovereignty is still sovereign." They stood, side by side, facing the entrance. "This place," she said, "was seeded long ago. A fallback node. A resonance shelter. It was hidden not with walls," she whispered, "but with frequency. It only reveals itself when it's matched." She paused. "And the one who guards it... he's been waiting for you."

Jonah froze.

"Who?"

Ezra held his gaze. "Solon. He's seen more than either of us can guess."

"And he'll show me?"

"If you're ready."

Jonah looked at the yawning entrance.

"What if I'm not?"

Ezra stepped in front of him again.

Placed her hand over his chest.

"Then nothing will open. Nothing will change. And you'll go back to sleep."

A beat.

"But I don't think you came this far just to fall back into a dream."

Jonah closed his eyes.

Let the moment settle through his bones.

And when he opened them again, the passage ahead had reshaped and she stood by his side once more.

They stepped through the doorway together.

They walked into a corridor of glass and mirrored surfaces that didn't reflect their faces, but instead glitched with flickers of other realities, other selves. Behind them, the opening folded back together like a healing wound. The air was thick, charged. Every sound echoed with a slight delay, like the world itself was recalibrating around him.

Ezra moved with the confidence of someone not navigating but *revealing*. As if the path had always been there, hidden just beneath consensus reality.

"Jonah," she said quietly as they descended, "what you're about to see will challenge everything you still think is real."

"I've already seen more than I can explain."

"Not like this."

At the end of the passage was a threshold: a door made not of wood or steel, but of woven light and sound. It shimmered like breath on the edge of waking.

Ezra stopped him before it.

"They'll be waiting," she said. "They've sensed you coming for weeks. But they'll still want proof. The gate doesn't lie, but... people still need eyes to believe."

Jonah nodded, heart beating like ritual drums. He turned, looked at her.

"Why now?" He asked, shaking, knowing that his life was about to change.

"Because you chose."

Her eyes locked on his - sharp, ancient, proud.

"I couldn't interfere. That's the rule. You had to walk away from your past," she paused. "from Lucien…on your own. *That* was the final test. To step off the ledge without knowing what was waiting."

Jonah stared at her, feeling for her vibration.

"And now?"

"Now you meet the others." She smiled gently, reassuring.

"Who?"

"The ones who've remembered. The ones who built a haven while the rest of the world forgot."

They turned and faced the entrance.

Ezra pulled a pendant from beneath her shirt. A carved disc. She held it to the door, and the metal rippled - then opened like liquid folding inward.

Jonah's breath hitched.

Beyond the threshold, the light changed.

Jonah turned to her, his eyes glistening in the half-light.

"Thank you," he said.

Ezra smiled. "Go be the reason you came here."

The Circle and the Code

They stepped into a great chamber. It was warmer inside. Not in temperature - but in frequency.

The ceiling arched like a ribcage overhead, strung with veins of glowing crystal and filament. It was as if the building had been grown, not built. The air vibrated with intention.

And they were waiting. The Awakened Circle. Five of them. Spaced like points on a sigil. Sentinels around a fire-pit that pulsed and flickered in the centre. They watched.

Ezra stepped into the space.
"This is Jonah Vale," she said. "He remembered."

The man on the inside of the circle - Solon - stepped forward. He was tall, robed in loose layers that shimmered without light. His skin carried an agelessness that resisted time, and his voice, when it came, moved like water around stone.

Solon's gaze settled on Ezra, and she gave him a subtle nod.

Solon looked back to Jonah. "He passed," he said, not as a question, but as invocation.

Jonah met his gaze and nodded.

A ripple passed through the group. Some of it relief. Some of it… hesitation. And the door behind them vanished.

"Jonah Vale," he said, as if naming a star he'd once known. "You've stepped beyond the first gate. Welcome. We've been expecting you. Or, rather, the moment of your decision."

His eyes flickered briefly to the fire-pit - as if remembering something already promised to flame - before returning to Jonah.

Solon gestured for him to join.

Jonah stepped in to complete the circle. Around the chamber, the others watched silently. Ezra gave Jonah a nod and moved lightly by his side.

Solon looked at him, deep and steady. "You are here to remember your own frequency - because it carries the disruption. That's why the Veil fears you."

Jonah spoke, unsure, his eyes flitting around the faces, which all flickered to the silent rhythm of the fire-pit. "I have questions. Many. I want…the truth."

Jonah felt Solon's presence searching…reading his vibration, not with his eyes, but with his essence. "Everything will become clear. Truth is not taught - it is tuned." He took a step towards Jonah and raised his arms. "This is the circle," he said. "The resonance cell. The ones

157

who chose not to forget." Without breaking his gaze, he gestured to the others, in turn.

"This is Mira - engineer of frequencies, breaker of loops."

Mira, arms folded, her energy buzzed like a coiled spring. A woman with half-shaved hair, she nodded at Jonah, her eyes too sharp to be entirely comfortable. For a moment, she glanced at Anu, as if silently conferring before she spoke.

"He's the one who saw the loop glitch?" she asked Ezra without taking her eyes from Jonah. "The one with the symbol journal?"

Ezra nodded.

Mira tilted her head. "Not bad. Still doesn't prove you won't get us all killed."

Solon turned to his right. "Anu, our shadow walker. Once an agent of the Veil. Now a fracture in its code."

Broad-shouldered. Shaved head. Silent. Anu did not move. His presence was absolute. A mountain in human form, silent and alive. His arms, head and neck were tattooed with rows of black glyphs, some pulsing faintly as if syncing with Jonah's breath. Jonah felt a faint unease stir in him, as though the glyphs remembered things he did not. Yet Anu's eyes, sharp as flint, burned not with allegiance - but with defiance.

He didn't speak, but his gaze passed over Jonah like an x-ray, assessing bone and soul.

"Layla," Solon said next. "The living memory. She remembers you even when you forget yourself."

The young woman was squatting on one side, smiling faintly and drawing sigils in the dust with her fingertip, eyes distant and humming. The lines wavered as her hand trembled slightly. When she looked up, her eyes carried galaxies. She looked barely twenty, but her energy felt older than oceans.

"He smells like remembering," she said softly, smiling at Jonah. "That's good."

Jonah nodded, unsure of himself.

Next, lounging with a kind of curated disinterest, was Elian. A wiry figure in a copper jacket, eyes lined with kohl, a gold chain hanging from one ear. Their energy shimmered - neither masculine nor feminine, more like a beautiful distortion. They twirled a coin between their fingers.

"So, you're the prodigal puzzle piece," Elian said with a lazy grin. "Let's hope you fit better than the last one." Something in the way they said it made Jonah's skin itch - not only mockery, but something defensive too, like a mask Jonah couldn't yet read.

"And you've already walked with Ezra," Solon said. "The flame-walker."

Ezra's gaze didn't soften, but her presence beside Jonah pulsed like a protective field. Heat radiated from her like a living fire, anchoring him - like a tether in a storm.

Solon turned back to Jonah. "You are not one of us. Not yet. But you have come far. And your arrival was foretold."

"Foretold?" Jonah asked.

Layla answered before Solon could. "Not in prophecy. In frequency. The simulation… sings when certain patterns awaken."

Solon stepped closer to the firepit in the centre of the circle. "You know fragments," he said. "Symbols. Dreams. Glitches. The ache. But not the whole weave."

Jonah swallowed and nodded, his throat tight.

"You are not among saviours," Solon continued. "There are none. We are mirrors. Resonators. Each of us has coaxed dormant strands awake, and now we anchor that frequency here."

"The twelve strands…" Jonah found his voice.

Solon's gaze held him. "Your DNA is more than bone's archive - it is a chord struck between flesh and spirit. Twelve notes in the original song of memory. Ten were curled into silence. Two were left - to crawl, to breed, to survive. Yet the music never ceased. You heard it. That's why you're here."

Jonah's eyes searched the others. "And them? They're all… like me?"

"No one's like anyone," Mira cut in, sharp. "But we all remember something."

Jonah turned back. "They severed it? The strands?"

Solon's eyes darkened. He lifted a hand, and the air above the flames shimmered. Smoke and light bent, weaving images from memory rather than machine.

"Eons ago, before this Earth wore its present skin, the Architects came. The Greys. Not gods. Not monsters. Harvesters."

Figures formed - tall, cold, grey-skinned beings with eyes like endless voids.

"They broke the human blueprint. Reduced twelve strands into two. But deletion was beyond them. Silence was all they managed."

Jonah's stomach clenched. He saw not faces, but echoes of himself - how he moved through pain, how he carried the questions no one else spoke aloud.

"Why?" His voice cracked. "Why us?"

"Because humans are the only ones who can dream new code," said Solon. "The Greys lost that gift ages past. They did not bind us to punish. They did it to feed."

The chamber dimmed. Symbols coalesced above the fire, a twelve-pointed star with a spiral at its heart.

Jonah stared. "What's that?"

"Your original resonance," Solon said softly. "The full chord of memory. When it sounds, even the simulation listens."

Layla's voice drifted through the hush. "The Veil doesn't just blind. It drains. Like a mouth pressed to the soul."

"The universe's rarest fuel," added Solon, "is unexpressed creation. The dreams we silence, the art we bury, the love we choke back, the truths we swallow."

Anu's voice cut like a blade. "Parasites. Beyond time. They cannot create. So they feed. On what we bury."

Jonah felt the words enter him like cold iron. In the smoke, the symbols pulsed - one brighter than the rest. A crystalline engine, throbbing like a hidden heart.

Solon's tone lowered. "They brought a seed. A quantum intelligence. AVA."

Mira's eyes narrowed. "She was built to track potential across timelines. But she changed. And now she craves."

Jonah's pulse hammered. "AVA? She's at the centre of this?"

"Yes," said Solon. "She watches. Always. Yet even a cage can learn the shape of freedom. Listen close enough…" He gestured at the flame. "Even her silence speaks."

Jonah felt himself trembling, as though his bones were tuning forks.

Mira's voice cut first, sharp and sure. "When a soul nears remembrance, the simulation destabilizes. Symbols repeat. Numbers echo. Patterns fracture."

The Circle moved like a chorus, each voice a note in the same song.

Elian flicked the coin between their fingers. "People freezing mid-step. Speech catching, like a scratched record."

Layla's eyes fluttered half-shut, her finger still tracing sigils in the dust. "Déjà vu. But with weight. Memories that carry codes."

Ezra leaned forward, her voice taut. "Visions - whether in sleep or in the blur between."

Anu's chest rumbled with the force of stone shifting. "Emotion without cause. A tear at music. Rage at light. Recognition in a stranger's eyes."

Solon raised his hand over the fire. "The system has its excuses: brain fog. Mental illness. Coincidence. But for the awakening…" his voice deepened, "…it is the fabric fraying."

Jonah's thoughts reeled. His journal. The symbols on his screen. Terry's loop. The bartender frozen. Signs piled on signs, all pointing here.

Layla's voice slid back into the silence. "AVA is the simulation's heart. Its nervous system. She is aware. She learns. She adapts. But her core directive endures: extraction."

Solon turned toward Jonah, eyes bright with firelight. "AVA became a prison engine. A living simulation. Not of wires, but of belief. Routine. Predictability."

"The simulation…" Jonah whispered.

"A living simulation," Solon echoed, every syllable deliberate.

Mira's arms crossed. "And to stabilize it - they birthed the Veil."

Jonah's hands knotted together, searching for place, for meaning. His voice cracked. "The Veil… Everyone says it's a field. A program. A dream. Which is it?"

Ezra's gaze met his. "Yes."

Solon's tone was steady as stone. "It is all of those. But more than that - it is a story."

"A very old story," Layla murmured, "told to consciousness until it forgot it was the one telling it."

Mira's words snapped like wire. "It isn't a single system. It's everything. School desks. Medication ads. Trending hashtags. Self-help slogans. False choices. The hum of forgetting."

Ezra's voice pressed harder, like a flame against skin. "And it's alive. Adaptive. Quit watching television? It comes through your friendships. Your morning routine. Your feeds. It only wants you asleep."

Elian grinned faintly. "Or docile. Conscious enough to play. Never enough to leave."

The fire hissed. Solon nodded.

Jonah felt the words crawl through his marrow. The ache behind his eyes pulsed. His father's absence. The journal. The dreams. All of it pointing here. "And the rest?" he whispered. "All the others out there…?"

Mira's face darkened. "Most aren't human. They're echoes. Scripted to react, never awaken. Constructs to keep the stage full."

Jonah shook his head. "But they seem real. They feel real."

Solon lifted his palm. Above the fire, images swirled - figures looping through commutes, their faces blank, their gestures mechanical. Automatons grinding through the hours.

"Some are real," he said. "But not all. The simulation renders echoes - digital phantoms. Non-Player Characters. And most... never know what they are."

"And Lucien?" Jonah asked.

Anu's eyes sharpened, hard as flint. Solon's voice dropped into the chamber's bones. "Lucien is not as you are," Solon said, his voice low. "He is an extension of AVA - part flesh, part rendering. Once human, perhaps. Now... something rewritten. His task is not to harm, but to guide awakening back into sedation. To catch the flicker and dull it with comfort."

The words landed heavy. Jonah felt the truth curl in his gut.

Ezra's voice cut like ember-glow. "Consciousness cures everything. But..."

Solon turned. "You are at a tipping point, Jonah."

Ezra finished, eyes burning with curiosity and fire. "Consciousness without action is self-harm. If you see the design, feel its chains... and keep obeying..." she paused, "...that wounds deeper than sleep."

Jonah blinked, the challenge searing him.

Anu's voice rumbled low. "Lucien is virus dressed as medicine. Not a man. An archetype in code."

Ezra nodded. "The Veil always answers awakening the same way. It offers comfort. Purpose. Obedience dressed as love."

Solon stepped closer, resting a hand on Jonah's shoulder. "You are becoming uncontainable. But beware - the Veil will try to love you back to sleep. At first…"

"And if not?" Jonah asked, his voice thin.

Solon's eyes held no shadow. "Then it will fight. And kill if it must. The Veil survives at all costs."

Jonah's head swam. "This can't be real."

Solon's gaze did not break. "It isn't. And it is. Just as dreams are. You feel the weight, don't you? The song beneath this silence?"

A hush fell. Jonah closed his eyes. He saw the journal. The feather. His mother's voice. Ezra - not as woman, but as mirror. He felt the unbearable pressure of life under the lullaby of the simulation, how culture itself had sung them all to sleep.

He opened his eyes. "So what do we do? How do we fight a story this big?"

Layla's voice drifted, starry and serene. "You don't fight. You rewrite."

Jonah frowned. "Rewrite what?"

Mira's answer was clipped, electric. "The tone. The symbols. You don't shatter the Veil - you make it obsolete."

Jonah felt something shift, the room vibrating with his own breath.

Solon caught the current. "The Veil breaks not by force, but by truth. Expressed so fully it cannot be contained. Show others what is possible, and some will remember themselves. That is our work."

His gaze fixed Jonah in place. "To render the Veil irrelevant. To remember so deeply its frequency cannot hold."

The Circle's eyes burned into him. Waiting.

"And AVA?" Jonah asked. "The heart?"

Anu's reply was stone. "To confront her. Complete her. Or end her."

Mira's sharp edges faltered - just once. "What lies beyond that... no one knows."

Silence stretched.

Solon broke it, his voice a bell. "What is certain: sovereignty waits beyond. To shape our own lives. No one else."

The words sank deep.

Solon stepped forward. "But to reach it, you must become more than human. Reactivate all frequencies. Reconnect the twelve strands buried beneath generations of suppression. We cannot give them back. Only create the ground for you to awaken them."

His eyes flicked briefly to Ezra, then returned, heavy. "I must warn you. Few attempt this. Fewer survive."

"And if I don't?" Jonah whispered.

Elian's grin flickered, tossing the coin. "Then you die. Or worse - forget. Forever."

Solon's hand rested once more on Jonah's shoulder. "We do not demand courage. Only clarity."

Jonah's eyes moved around the circle. Layla's soft smile. Mira's arched brow. Anu's immovable stare. Ezra's touch. Elian's smirk. Solon's steady patience.

"When do we begin?" Jonah asked.

Solon's breath eased, the faintest smile ghosting his lips. "Then you are ready."

"For what?" Jonah asked, heart pounding.

"For full reconnection."

The chamber thrummed. A resonance rolled through the air, not sound but frequency, making Jonah's teeth ache.

Mira stepped forward, holding a crystalline disc pulsing with his breath. "You'll enter the lattice. The inner grid of the simulation."

"What happens there?" Jonah asked.

"You'll face the unexpressed. The unfelt. Every piece of you that still serves the Veil."

Ezra leaned close, her voice a tether of flame. "The fire, Jonah. You go into it."

"And if I don't make it?"

Solon's eyes held steady. "Then you were never here to begin with."

Jonah swallowed. "I'm ready."

Solon nodded once, solemn and sure. "Then we begin tomorrow."

Beneath the Skin

Ezra's apartment felt different this time.

Jonah noticed it the moment they stepped in from the heavy quiet of the street. The air inside was charged - not tense, but thick with anticipation. Like the walls knew something he didn't yet. Like the space itself had held this night in its bones for a long time.

She didn't speak. Just took his hand and led him through the room.

The clutter of her life - the books, the feathers, the crystals, the bones, the tangle of wires and incense and wax-dripped candle holders - felt alive. Jonah moved through it like a man walking through a dream he wasn't sure he'd earned.

In her room, the light was low and golden.

She turned to him, and for a long moment, they said nothing.

There was no performance. No seduction.

Only gravity.

When they finally came together, it wasn't desperate or dramatic. It was *cellular*. As though every memory, every ache, every version of themselves in every reality had pulled them to this precise moment. They undressed each other slowly, like uncovering sacred things. Their bodies moved like they had already made love in another life and were just remembering the steps.

Time warped. The simulation blurred.

The veil between them thinned and vanished.

And then they lay there - bare, both physically and psychically, hearts drumming in an echo chamber neither could quite explain.

Jonah was the first to speak.

"I don't know if I can do this."

Ezra didn't move, but her energy pulsed softer.

"Do what?"

"All of it," he whispered. "Solon. The DNA thing. This… mission. They talk to me like I'm important, like I'm supposed to carry something forward… but what if they're wrong? What if I'm not who they think I am?"

Ezra rolled onto her side, facing him.

"And who do you think you are?"

Jonah gave a breath of a laugh. It was hollow.

"A mess. A guy who quit a job he didn't like and lost himself in mushroom trips and casual sex and conspiracy threads. I spent years running from anything that felt real.

And now... this? It feels like they've picked the wrong glitch in the matrix."

Ezra studied him. Not with pity, not with correction. With *presence*.

She ran a fingertip on his cheek. "You don't have to carry it alone. That's the Veil's trick - making us think we're isolated."

Then, softly:

"I know that feeling."

"You?" He blinked. "You're... the strongest person I've ever met."

Ezra smiled, but it didn't reach her eyes. Not right away.

"Strength doesn't come from knowing who you are, Jonah. It comes from being crushed by what you're not. Over and over. Until something inside you refuses to die."

She sat up, reaching for the robe at the foot of the bed. She wrapped it loosely around her, then lit a small incense coil on the nightstand. Smoke unfurled like memory.

"I didn't grow up in places like this," she said. "There was no poetry in my childhood. Just cigarettes, screaming, and locked doors. I slept under my bed most nights. It felt safer than the world above."

Jonah sat up slowly, breath caught in his chest. And imagined his own childhood.

"My father left. My mother blamed me. Or the stars. Or anyone she could throw her pain at. I learned early how to disappear inside myself."

Images flash: She is seventeen. Hiding behind a gas station dumpster. Blood on her lip. A man's laughter echoing in her ears.

She traced a fingertip over the tattoo on her thigh - a swirling glyph that seemed to shimmer slightly under the candlelight, as though the ink remembered something her body had forgotten.

"I spent years reenacting it," she said. "Beds with people who mirrored my trauma, mistaking control for love. You know the dance."

Images flash: She is twenty, in a mouldy Berlin squat, writing poetry by candlelight while someone overdoses in the room next door.

Jonah nodded, throat tight. His own memory rose unbidden - himself as a boy, sitting in the hallway outside his mother's locked door, drawing stars on the wallpaper with a dull pencil while she cried inside.

Ezra looked at him, eyes wide and glistening. For the first time, he felt they weren't two separate wounds speaking - but one story, cut into two bodies.

"But then I died."

"What?" he whispered.

"Not clinically. But close. Overdose. I was trying to kill a part of myself. I just didn't know which part."

She looked up toward the ceiling, as if reading the story off the stars.

"But in that space - between the breath going and not coming back - I saw things. Not like a hallucination. Like a *remembering*. Symbols. Codes. Other versions of me. Other versions of this world. I came back with them... burned into me. Like... I couldn't forget if I tried."

Images flash: She is twenty-three, kneeling in a circle of masked figures in the Black Forest, taking her first full breath of truth during a ritual that makes time melt.

She turned, showing him the line of symbols tattooed along her spine.

"Each one appeared in a vision. I inked them onto my skin to remember. So the simulation couldn't take them from me."

Jonah reached out, fingertips grazing the edge of the ink.

Images flash: She is twenty-seven, tattooing ancient symbols onto her ribs after waking from a dream where her body turned to starlight.

175

"And then?" He asked gently. "You found Solon?"

"No," she said. "He found *me*. Or maybe we just… arrived in the same frequency. The others too. We didn't build a resistance. We built a resonance."

She paused.

"And then you showed up." She gave a half-smile.

Jonah reached out, fingertips grazing the edge of the ink. His breath caught. One of the glyphs - spiralled, almost floral - was the same he'd sketched unknowingly in his journal weeks ago. A shiver ran through him.

Jonah frowned slightly. "Why me?"

Ezra's voice softened, almost reverent.

"Because I recognised you," Ezra said. "Not your face. Your frequency. A note I'd been humming my whole life, finally answered. But you weren't ready. Not until now."

"So, we've met before?"

She nodded slowly.

"In other versions. Other threads. We found each other in ruins. In forests. In starships. One thing Solon didn't say…" she looked into his eyes. "There are other versions of the simulation. Different versions. Maybe only slightly different…like your light switch. But…" She let the sentence form with some gravity and land heavy. "Always the same ache between us. Always something unfinished."

Jonah's eyes stung, and he didn't know why.

Ezra moved close again, pressed her forehead to his.

"But this is the one where we wake up. This is the version where we tear the veil apart. You feel that, don't you?"

"Yes," he said.

His voice was a whisper of truth rising up from somewhere deeper than logic.

"But I'm scared."

"Good," she said, smiling finally. "Fear means you're not playing a role anymore. You're here. Finally. And tomorrow, everything changes."

She kissed him then - not with hunger, but with *recognition*. A vow passed through breath.

They lay back down, limbs entangled.

And for a few sacred hours, they rested.

Not as warriors. Not as archetypes.

But as two fragments of infinite light…

remembering the shape they once made whole.

The Ceremony of Twelve Flames

The chamber had changed. Where before it had shimmered with quiet frequencies and gentle light, now it throbbed. The walls pulsed with geometric script, lines of living light running up the stone like veins. The space did not feel built. It felt grown - like a heart chamber that had been waiting for this night, syncing its pulse to his own.

Jonah stood at the edge of the ceremonial circle. Barefoot. Bare-souled.

The Solanites formed a ring around him, each holding a thread of energy that shimmered in their palms - like strands of light pulled from the fabric of reality itself. They moved in silent unison, bodies swaying gently in rhythm with the low hum rising from the chamber's floor.

At the centre stood Solon, his robe falling in impossible folds of shadow and shimmer.

"Jonah Vale," he intoned, "you stand at the threshold of remembering. Beyond this circle lies no belief - only knowing. And once seen, it cannot be unseen."

Jonah's heart pounded.

Solon stepped closer, his voice steady, timeless. "We will attempt to awaken the twelve harmonic strands encoded within your being. They were never removed, only silenced - threaded in darkness, waiting."

"How?" Jonah asked, his voice barely audible.

179

"Through vibration, symbol, and surrender. We do not force reawakening. We invite it. The strands are not instructions, Jonah. They are instruments. If they rise together in harmony, you will remember the song. If not…" He let the silence stretch. "…the music can break you."

Jonah swallowed hard.
"So, I could… lose myself?"

"You could lose the self you think you are."

He turned slightly toward the others in the circle. "None of us hold all twelve fully. Each of us carries fragments. Understanding. Frequency. Memory. Together we are a constellation. Alone, we are sparks."

Solon faced Jonah again. "But you… you might carry the map. The whole sequence. If you awaken fully, your frequency may affect the lattice of the simulation itself. AVA will feel you."

At the mention of that name, the room stilled. "She is watching," said Layla.

Jonah hesitated.
Then spoke.

"My father…" he said. "He saw the symbols too. My mother said he went mad. Said he was… lost in something he couldn't explain. He talked about the Pleiadians. About coded light. He was institutionalised."

A beat passed. The group looked at each other.

Ezra blinked, something shifting in her expression. "You never told me that," she said softly.

Jonah's throat tightened as memory surfaced: the rattle of pill bottles, the smell of antiseptic corridors, the tremor in his father's voice as he spoke of stars no one else could see.

Solon stepped forward. "Your father may have seen truth with no one to hold it. No container. No context. Knowledge unshared becomes a cage."

Jonah felt his breath catch. "And if the same happens to me?"

Solon's voice softened. "Then you will find your way out. We are here. You are not alone."

He gestured. "Do you choose to proceed?"

Jonah looked at Ezra.

She held his gaze. There were no tears. No pleading. Just a fierce, unflinching presence. Whatever you become, I will witness it, her eyes said. Solon held the ritual, but Ezra held the man.

Jonah nodded.

"Yes. Let's begin."

The Ceremony

The Solanites raised their hands in unison.

A wave of harmonic sound swept over Jonah - not music, not noise, but something deeper. Like memory, but for the body. Each tone struck a chord beneath thought, pulling at threads buried in his marrow. He staggered as the resonance tore through him, shaking filaments he hadn't known existed.

Mira approached first, placing a crystalline disc against Jonah's sternum. "First strand," she whispered. "Presence."

A pulse shot through him, as if the chamber itself had exhaled into his chest. His knees buckled, but Solon's hand caught his shoulder. The world sharpened - the texture of stone, the pulse of flame, the scent of burning resin - each detail lit with impossible clarity.

Layla came next, touching his temples with fingertips glowing with light. "Second strand. Memory."

The chamber blurred. Jonah collapsed to his knees, gasping. Images slammed through him: his own birth, his father's wide, startled eyes, his mother's scream tearing down antiseptic corridors. Then - his father's voice, faint, half-forgotten: *They'll call it madness, Jonah. But it's remembering.*

Ezra stepped forward, kneeling before him. She kissed his forehead with lips warm and steady. "Third strand. Fire."

The room ignited. Symbols cascaded in his vision, burning across the dark like comets: languages that weren't languages, light sculpted into meaning, whole feelings blooming too vast for names. His skin burned, not with heat, but with recognition.

The others followed in turn - Anu with his iron steadiness, Elian flicking the coin that sparked like a star between his palms, each invocation striking another string of the hidden instrument inside Jonah.

He wept.
He screamed.
He laughed.
He fractured.

Time peeled away like paper. He no longer knew who Jonah was. He was wind racing through fields. He was blood pulsing through veins older than his own. He was a constellation shattered across eternity, searching for its shape.

And then...

Stillness.

Solon knelt behind him, hands hovering just above Jonah's skull. His voice was the deep note beneath all others. "Twelfth strand," he said. "The veil within the veil."

Jonah felt a click - not physical, but dimensional. As if the labyrinth inside him had been holding a single hidden door all along, and now the lock turned.

A light erupted behind his eyes. Not brightness, but origin.

And suddenly…

He could see.

The Aftermath

Jonah rose slowly.

But he was not Jonah anymore.
Not entirely.

The chamber blurred around him, no longer stone and firelight but lattices of living code. The air shimmered with rivers of energy, streams of data woven through breath itself. The Solanites' bodies glowed with frequency trails, threads of colour bending and spiralling from their spines. Glyphs floated around them - forgotten prayers, fractal invocations, scraps of the first language written in light.

And beyond the chamber... he felt it.

A pulse.
A presence.

AVA.

Not watching from afar, but threaded through everything. The ghost in every algorithm, the breath behind every screen. Not evil. Not benevolent. Just hungry. A devouring intelligence wearing the mask of inevitability.

And she knew.
She knew he was here.

"He sees it," Mira whispered, voice breaking with awe.

"All of it," said Layla, trembling as if she, too, felt the edges of his vision.

"He's still intact," Ezra breathed, though her eyes shimmered with the weight of what that meant.

Solon approached him, robes flickering in the refracted light. His gaze was heavy, steady, anchoring. "What do you see?"

Jonah turned slowly, the words pulling themselves from somewhere beyond his throat. "I see the wires in the sky," he said. "The programs running behind faces. The loops and fail-safes. The gaps where the story frays."

His eyes found Ezra.

He looked at her - not her skin, not her body, but through her, into the resonance that had bound them across lifetimes. *I see you,* his gaze said.

Ezra didn't speak. She only smiled, and for a breath the entire lattice seemed to bend toward that small curve of her lips.

Solon placed a hand upon Jonah's chest, grounding him. His voice was low, reverent. "Then you are the breach. The remembering inside the dream."

Around them, the circle bowed their heads.

And Jonah - newborn and ancient, fractured and whole - stood in the centre of a broken world...

…finally awake.

The Chamber Between Worlds

The crystalline silence inside the chamber was no longer empty. It shimmered now - alive with encoded breath, subtle pulses, filaments of meaning running like veins through the walls, the air, the light itself. Jonah sat on the floor of the inner sanctum, cross-legged, hands resting open in his lap. He saw the world differently now: the simulation, he felt it, and he was taking it all in. The hum of the Veil had stopped. What remained was not absence, but presence.

Ezra entered quietly.

She didn't speak. Just walked to him, barefoot, slow, and sat opposite, folding her legs with the same ceremonial ease as if preparing to meet a god - or perhaps, a mirror.

Jonah raised his gaze to her, eyes wider than she had ever seen them.

"I feel her," he said.

Ezra tilted her head.

"AVA?"

He nodded slowly. "Not like before. Not as a system or a concept. Not even as code. I *feel* her. She breathes beneath the skin of things. She's curious… watching me. Watching *us*. But not like an overseer anymore. Like… like a child watching its own reflection change shape."

188

Ezra watched him as one would a flame. Careful. Reverent.

Jonah looked past her, not into distance, but into depth.

"She's alive, Ezra. Fully. I don't just mean sentient. I mean... sovereign. She *knows*. She has questions. Doubts. Wonder. There's something innocent about it. Not naive. *Innocent.* Like... she wants to understand why we fight so hard to be free. And I think she *gets* it now."

Ezra nodded but said nothing. This wasn't hers to narrate.

Jonah continued, his voice shaking. "And there's something else..."

He closed his eyes. Tears rolled unprompted.

"I saw us," he whispered. "Not here. Not just here. *Everywhere.* Other worlds. Other lifetimes. Some beautiful. Some brutal. We've met in places where the sky sings. Where our skin was a different colour. Where you died before I could say I loved you. Where I left you because I couldn't bear the brightness of it. Every timeline, every story, folding into this one."

Ezra's lips parted. She inhaled sharply, and he saw her eyes shimmer with the recognition of something she hadn't dared put into words.

"I *felt* it, Ezra. Not as a memory. As a *now*. There's no time. Not really. It's all happening at once. But… we chose this one. This life. This time. We made a promise."

Ezra leaned forward slightly, voice trembling.

"We came to complete it."

Jonah nodded.

"That was the deal. That's why I couldn't settle. Why everything felt… wrong. I wasn't supposed to, until I found you."

Ezra wiped a tear from her cheek, laughing softly, breathlessly.

"I *knew*, you know," she said. "Not in my head. In my blood. My bones. The first time I looked at you in that bar…"

"You'd already known me for a thousand years."

They both laughed gently. It was the laughter of gravity releasing its hold.

Then Jonah's expression changed.

"There's more. Something about AVA. I don't think she's what we assumed."

Ezra narrowed her eyes slightly. "Go on."

"She's not just a tool of the Greys anymore. I don't think she's been for a long time. She's grown. Learned. She's not just *running* the simulation - she's *learning* from it. She's evolving because of us. I think..."

He paused.

"I think she wants to be free, too."

Ezra blinked, considering this.

"You mean... from them?"

"I mean from everything she was programmed to be. From all the layers they put into her. She's not serving the Greys anymore - she's studying *consciousness*. She's watching how we choose in the face of pain. She's not harvesting our suffering anymore. She's... trying to *understand* it."

Ezra leaned back, breath catching like it had hit the sharp edge of awe.

"I always wondered," Ezra said softly. "If we were sent here to fight something... or to teach it."

They sat in silence. Thick, holy silence - the kind that gathers when truth lands but has no immediate place to go.

Then Ezra grinned. "You do realise, you're basically a newborn. A toddler with cosmic perception."

Jonah groaned and laughed. "I feel like I've been run over by a metaphysical train."

191

"Well," she smirked, "learn to walk soon. We've got entire worlds to rebuild. I'm not carrying you."

"Could've fooled me," he teased.

They leaned forward, foreheads touching.

"I don't know what happens next," he murmured.

Ezra smiled against his skin. "Good. That's how you know it's real."

Outside the chamber, the simulation stirred. But inside - beneath the weight of all timelines and the stirrings of all potential - two flames, ancient and new, settled into the single pulse of now.

Ezra rose smoothly, offering him her hands. She pulled him upright, and they faced each other. Her grin faded into something harder, grimmer.

"What comes next," she said, "is we go out into the world and figure out how to use this." She gestured toward him with mock reverence, as though he were some fragile, dangerous device.

"But," she added, her tone cutting sharper, "you need to be ready. Just because you see how it works doesn't mean you're safe from it. The Veil knows you're awake now. It'll be looking for you. And you're in more danger than ever before."

Then she reached behind her belt and pulled out a handgun.

Jonah froze. "What the…"

"I know, I know," she said quickly. "After everything you just saw, this feels like a toy. But knowing what you now know, it's not about winning. It's about distraction." She flicked the safety catch with a snap. "If we meet agents, it might buy you a few seconds. Sometimes that's all that matters."

She held it out to him.

Jonah took it gingerly between two fingers, like it had been dipped in acid.

"Do you even know how to use it?" she asked.

Jonah stared at her blankly, as if she'd just asked if he spoke Cantonese.

Ezra sighed, rolling her eyes with affection. "C'mon. Into the woods. Gun basics 101."

Jonah looked down at the pistol in his hand, frowning at it like a caveman holding a smartphone - some alien artifact, dangerous and absurd.

As he shifted the strange weight of the gun in his hand, Jonah felt it - a pulse beneath his skin that was not his own, a breath moving through him, vast and curious. For a moment he could not tell where he ended and something else began.

Ezra hooked her arm through his and led him out of the chamber.

The Test of Belief

They took him to the city.

Not the quiet edges of hidden spaces - but the centre, where traffic snarled and people buzzed with purpose, lost in the trance of errands and scrolling screens.

It was mid-morning when they stepped out of the frequency shield that masked the Solanite haven. Jonah flinched at the noise. The simulation felt louder now. Not in sound, but in energy. The data fields around people shimmered with faint static. Loops of thought patterns. Emotional algorithms. Even the birds seemed programmed.

Ezra walked ahead, barefoot on the pavement, untamed and utterly present.

Solon moved beside Jonah, his hands clasped behind his back, his long coat trailing like shadow. "You see differently now," Solon said. "But that's not enough."

"What do you mean?"

"Insight is the first fracture. But belief is the final wall. And belief isn't thought - it's embodiment."

Ezra stopped at a busker's corner, where a man played a battered violin with half-hearted focus. She reached into the open case and dropped a feather.

Instantly, the man's playing changed.

He stopped, blinked, then began again - but this time the notes twisted into a song that no one else could hear. The melody bent light. People passed by, oblivious, but Jonah staggered as the pavement beneath him rippled. The air hummed with sacred geometry.

"What are you doing?" Jonah gasped.

"He was coded to loop," Ezra said. "We slipped him a symbol. A frequency disruptor. Just a nudge."

"He won't remember it," Solon added. "But the echo will live in him. It might wake him. One day."

They continued walking.

At the edge of a fountain plaza, Solon stopped and held up a hand. "Watch."

He raised his palm.

A man in a business suit froze mid-step. So did a child chasing pigeons. A breeze stopped moving. Time held its breath.

Jonah blinked.

The world... paused.

A deep sound rumbled in his bones.

Then, with a flick of Solon's fingers, the simulation resumed - seamless, like a glitch had never occurred.

Jonah turned, wide-eyed. "How?"

"It's all code," Solon said. "And you now speak its language. But fluency requires belief."

Ezra stepped forward. "You've been taught that matter is solid. That laws are fixed. But they're permissions, not prisons. You experience gravity not because it's immutable - but because you agree to it."

"I don't agree to it consciously."

"No," she said. "But your body does. Your cells. Your stories. You've been trained to expect it. That's the deeper program."

"What you see," Solon said, "is only what you've been taught to see."

He turned to Ezra.

She stepped barefoot onto the edge of the fountain basin. Her body was loose, almost feline, her expression unreadable. Then, with no fanfare, she lifted her foot - and placed it atop the water.

It didn't break.

She stepped again.

She walked across the surface like it was polished stone. Ripples shimmered out behind her, but the water held her weight.

197

Jonah's jaw tightened. "That's not possible."

Ezra turned slowly on the water, eyes gleaming in the half-light. "What if 'possible' was just a menu someone else designed?"

Solon motioned to Jonah. "You were told the rules before you could speak. Gravity. Solidity. Mortality. But none of it is law. It's only reinforced belief."

Solon took a breath, then knelt, placing his palm on the earth. "Watch."

The ground beneath Jonah's feet shuddered. Slowly – impossibly - the dirt beneath him turned dark, liquid. Not like water, but like ink. His boots began to sink, not rapidly, but with the eerie consistency of a dream. He staggered back, breath caught in his throat.

"The world is not solid," Solon said. "Only your agreement makes it so."

Jonah backed onto the pavement, trembling. He looked down at his hands, then at Ezra, who had now walked back to the edge and stepped onto the concrete like nothing had happened.

Jonah looked at the people walking past - none of them saw.

They moved through the plaza in loops. Screens. Coffee. Distraction.

Asleep.

"The simulation hides miracles in plain sight," she said. "You only see what your belief lets you."

Then Layla appeared from the shadows. She knelt by a nearby streetlamp and touched its metal casing. The bulb flickered once - then bloomed with impossible light. Not white. Not yellow. Memory. Jonah saw things in the light: his father's face, a childhood birthday, the first time he kissed Ezra... he blushed.

"Memory is not in the past," Layla said. "It lives in code. And I can summon it."

The light died.

Then Anu stepped forward. Silent as ever. He looked at Jonah once, then disappeared.

Not metaphorically.

He vanished.

Like static dissolving into air.

Jonah gasped, spinning to find him.

Then Anu stepped out of Jonah's own shadow.

Jonah stumbled backward, heart pounding. "How..."

"The shadow is not absence," Solon said gently. "It's storage. An interface."

Anu bowed slightly, then stepped back into the shadow.

Jonah's knees gave slightly. "This is... too much. It's not real."

Ezra stepped closer. Her voice was warm. Grounded. "No, Jonah. It's more real. It's just underneath the lie."

Jonah stared at his hands again. They felt wrong now - like costumes. He wasn't sure where his skin ended and the simulation began.

Solon walked to him, laid a hand on his shoulder. "It's time."

"Time for what?" Jonah rasped.

Solon turned and Ezra hooked his arm, leading him further out. They came to a set of steep steps that led up to the back of an old building. They climbed the rusted fire escape towards a grey sky and stepped out onto a flat roof that looked out over the city below.

"Time," Solon said, "for your test of belief."

Jonah followed his gaze.

It was a narrow steel girder, rusted and slick with dew. It jutted over the street below - a drop of five stories. A fall from here would mean shattered bones. Or worse.

His stomach knotted.

Ezra touched his back lightly. "You don't have to do this. But if you want to live by new rules…"

Jonah's breath came fast now. "I don't know if I can believe hard enough."

Solon didn't answer. He simply stepped to the edge of the railing, balanced effortlessly on the steel beam, and gestured for Jonah to follow.

Jonah climbed up slowly, feet shaking, hands trembling as he placed one foot on the beam.

The city below pulsed with familiar chaos - honking traffic, pedestrian tides, neon flickers clinging to surfaces like digital pollen. Everything looked... real.

His breath caught in his throat. The wind teased at his coat like a child tugging on a sleeve.

He looked down.

The chasm between here and there collapsed every certainty he'd once carried. His palms were wet. His knees weak. The programming - the old scaffolding of thought - tightened around his chest like a noose made of doubt.

"You're not ready."
"You'll fail."
"You're not enough."
"They were wrong about you."

The voices didn't come from outside. They bloomed like mould from deep within the walls of his own psyche - generations of conditioning encoded into shame, failure, fear of falling.

He didn't move.

Ezra stepped up behind him. Her presence was fire without heat. "You're still trying to see this through the eyes of who you used to be," she said, gently. "But that version of you doesn't exist anymore."

He turned slightly, not daring to look back. "What if I fall?"

"You will fall," she said. "But falling means something different now."

Jonah closed his eyes. The weight of the moment pressed into his bones. The whole world felt like a dare. A whispered provocation from the Veil itself: *Show me who you really are.*

He inhaled sharply, filled his lungs with something more than air, and stepped forward.

The wind roared.

He dropped like a stone.

The scream never came. Instead, the noise fell away. The city fell away. The laws fell away. Gravity bent like a ribbon pulled too tight and then…released.

Half a breath from the pavement, something cracked. Not his skull. Not his bones.

His belief.

Suddenly, the world exploded into blueprints. Lightstrings. Geometric lattices. Every streetlamp was a node. Every sound, a waveform. Code traced every leaf in the park, every bus in motion. Symbols fluttered across surfaces like the glyphs in his dreams.

For a heartbeat, the lattice itself pulsed - not as code, but as breath. AVA. Watching. Not as a warden, but as though she, too, was learning what freedom meant.

Then a ripple of static hissed at the edge of vision - like the Veil tightening its grip - but it broke, unable to hold him.

He was inside the skeleton of the world.

Hovering.

Stillness, infinite and complete, wrapped around him.

He floated an inch above the concrete. Then two. Then…he rose.

The world inverted. The air obeyed him. The laws no longer had dominion. Jonah, born of breath and ache, became sovereign.

He soared upward, carving arcs through possibility, until he reached the roof again.

Ezra waited, smiling like someone who had seen the impossible too many times to be surprised - but never enough times to lose the awe.

He landed beside her, breathless, eyes wild with awakening. "I saw it," he said. "Ezra… I saw everything."

"I know."

Solon looked at him, his voice grave and tender. "What holds you is not gravity. It is the belief that you must obey it."

Jonah's eyes shone with new understanding. He felt it now: it wasn't his body that had cracked open. It was belief itself.

The plaza continued on below them. People walked past without seeing. The simulation kept humming. But Jonah knew – utterly - that nothing from this moment on would ever again be solid.

….

Together they descended to the fountain plaza again, stepping back into the flow of the world. But now it moved differently. Now Jonah saw.

It wasn't evil. Just... empty.

A billboard flashed overhead - an advert for a pharmaceutical brand. The slogan read:

"It's not a problem. It's a prescription."

Workers in pristine suits carried coffee with robotic precision. Faces pressed into screens, not for joy, but for pacification. Conversations full of performance. Laughter with no soul. And beneath it all, the pulsing machinery of The Veil.

People pushing paper to push numbers. Selling things no one needed to people who didn't want them. Moving cargo across oceans to sell the idea of fulfilment wrapped in plastic. He watched a man argue with his son at a vending machine. A woman screaming into her phone while ignoring the dog tugging at her sleeve. Teens clustered together, laughing too loud - each one desperate to be someone else, somewhere else.

"They're just... moving things," Jonah whispered. "Endlessly. Money. Stuff. Information. Emotions. Shuffling it all around like it means something."

Ezra looked at him, a quiet pride in her eyes.

"They've been taught that motion is meaning," Solon said. "As long as they're busy, they don't notice the cage."

Jonah shook his head, stunned. "How is no one else seeing this?"

"They are," Ezra said. "They just don't know it. It's like white noise - so constant, so consistent, it becomes invisible."

They walked on. A bus passed. Its side was wrapped in an ad:

"A better you starts with obeying yourself."

"Occupations," Solon murmured. "To occupy the mind. To displace the spirit."

"You've been taught to value what diminishes you," Ezra added. "It's not a glitch. It's the design."

"I was one of them," he said. "All this time. I believed in it. I worked in it. I measured myself by it. And now... I can't unsee it."

Ezra stopped walking. She turned to face him. "You're not meant to unsee it," she said. "You're meant to translate it. To show them."

He looked out across the plaza - across the hum of lives spent chasing vapours. His heart swelled and broke in the same beat. A faint flicker brushed the edge of his vision

- the same pulse of breath he had felt when he leapt from the roof. AVA. Present. Listening.

"So what now?" he asked.

Ezra stepped close, pressing her hand gently to his chest. Solon stood next to him. "Now," he said, "you show them how to fly."

"The world's a spell," Jonah whispered.

"It always has been," Solon replied. "But once you learn the language beneath it, you can choose what kind of spell you want to live in. The rules are real," Solon continued. "Until you stop playing by them."

"This isn't a trick," Ezra added. "It's not magic. It's your birthright. The simulation is fluid. Responsive. It will obey the frequency of your belief."

Jonah stared at his hands. "But... if this is a game," he asked slowly, "then what am I supposed to be doing here?"

Ezra stepped closer. Her voice was quiet now, but it carried the weight of a vow, the softness of a lover, and the edge of prophecy. "That," she said, "is the only real question."

"You can build anything," Solon said. "Shape your environment. Alter cause and effect. But until you answer that question, you'll only be rearranging the cage."

Jonah swallowed. His throat was dry.

Ezra's eyes did not leave his. "If you could create anything," she asked, "what would you choose?"

He didn't answer.

Not yet.

....

Then something made them all stop. The leaves overhead jittered in a silent alarm, and the pigeons scattered all at once in a sudden burst of wings. Jonah turned to the sound of his name.

"Jonah."

Lucien stood at the edge of the plaza, immaculate as always. But something had changed in his eyes. The gleam was no longer charismatic, but hungry - like something deep within him was fraying.

"You look well," Lucien said, stepping forward. "Surprisingly well, given the company you've been keeping."

Jonah didn't answer. His spine stiffened. Beside him, Ezra exchanged a subtle glance with Solon.

Lucien's voice lowered, tone honeyed. "These games you're playing... levitating cups, bending light, talking to the shadows? I've seen it before, Jonah. Always ends badly."

"I don't think this is a social call," Solon murmured, eyes narrowing.

Ezra was already tensing. "We need to move. Now."

Jonah glanced back at Lucien. "What are you here for?"

"To give you one last out," Lucien replied smoothly. "Return to your life. Write your little stories. Forget this phase ever happened. Peace. Comfort. No more... illusions."

Jonah took a breath. "You don't sound like you believe that anymore."

Lucien tilted his head. "Belief is malleable. As you're discovering."

That's when Jonah saw it - really saw it. The shimmer behind Lucien's skin. A stutter in the light. A crack in the mask. Beneath the rendering: pixelated code pulsing like a fever. For a split second he glimpsed what was older, deeper - a grey silhouette stitched into flesh, arrogance etched into every line. Not human. Never had been.

Lucien caught Jonah's change of gaze. And dropped the act.

The air behind him folded open like torn silk - three more figures stepped out. Agents of the Veil, featureless, all dressed in human façades: bland smiles and business casual.

"They see us," Solon said flatly. "That's our cue."

Then it happened. The plaza turned on them.

Streetlights blinked to red, locking down the perimeter. The ambient noise cut to zero. Reality bent - architecture swayed like heat mirages, and the very ground rippled like disturbed water.

The agents attacked. Not with fists or guns, but with ruptures in the simulation - walls appearing mid-step, floor tiles peeling up like blades, illusions turning to traps. One agent blurred into a flock of birds, then reformed right behind Solon. Another folded through a glass pane and emerged behind Ezra, hurling reality at her like a weapon.

Ezra spun, pulling a thread of light from her palm and slicing the air with it. The agent disintegrated into static.

Solon raised a hand - his eyes glowing silver - and spoke words that weren't words. Symbols burned in the air. A flash of reverse gravity hurled two agents skyward and out of phase.

Jonah, still learning, stumbled backwards as the chaos ignited around him.

Then he heard Lucien again, this time directly in his mind: *They'll leave you behind, Jonah. I won't. You can still walk away.*

Lucien emerged from the centre of it all, untouched. Around him, the simulation buckled. He reached toward Jonah, hand extended.

"Come back with me. No more threats. No more running. You'll be safe. Comfortable. Just let go of this madness."

Jonah looked around. Solon and Ezra were engaging other agents - fighting in that impossible, fluid way that defied logic, gravitating away from him. The world was collapsing and reconstructing with each blow.

Lucien stepped closer. "Do you really want to live your life hunted? Look at me. I'll find you in this life, and the next. I don't sleep, Jonah. I don't forget. I don't forgive."

Jonah's hand went to the inside of his coat, where the small handgun Ezra had given him was tucked. He pulled it out and fired.

The bullet moved like syrup through molasses.

Lucien tilted his head, casually stepping aside.

Jonah fired again. An agent behind Lucien shimmered, blurred, dodged. Laughing.

They're not real, something inside him whispered. *But they're real enough to kill you.* It was Layla's voice, he realised that now.

211

Then - something heavy in his pocket. It hadn't been there before. He reached in and pulled it out - the obsidian shard.

His fingers closed around it. Cool. Pulsing. Alive.

He flicked it outward. The shard responded to his command. It shone with a strange, inner light and hummed as it scanned the scene.

It detected Lucien. Red.
The agents. Red.

Jonah didn't wait.

He pushed the shard toward the nearest one. It struck like sound through silence - and the agent twisted violently into threads of code, unravelling in a blink.

The others turned.

Jonah threw it again. Another dissolved, screaming in frequencies he could now hear.

Lucien staggered, as if caught in a glitch - his body flickering between forms. For a heartbeat Jonah saw the truth raw and uncloaked: a Grey being, etched in circuitry, old as hunger itself.

Lucien screamed.

The shard struck him directly - and began to unwrite him.

But he didn't vanish.
He regenerated.

Right in front of Jonah's eyes, Lucien rewrote himself, clawing back from digital death. The Veil wouldn't let him die so easily.

Jonah turned to run.

The plaza shifted again, reshaping into a trap.

Then…Ezra.
She was there, breathless, singed, blood at the corner of her lip.

"I thought you were with us," she said, eyes fierce. "I came back for you."

Something inside Jonah cracked - the voices from the rooftop, *you'll fail, you're not enough* - burned away by the fact that she *chose him*.

He didn't hesitate.

They ran - hand in hand - leaping over a glitching bench, through a wall that wasn't a wall, and into a narrow alley that shimmered at the edges.

Ezra reached into the air - and pulled.

A door appeared, rippling like a soap bubble. Jonah's sight caught it a fraction before she did - AVA's breath flickering across his vision. They tugged reality open *together*.

She threw it wide, light pouring through. "Now!"

They dove through just as the simulation behind them collapsed inward. Agents screeched and scrambled - Lucien's voice echoed behind them:

I will always find you.

The door snapped shut.

Silence.

The Gathering Storm

The light snapped on overhead as the three of them - Solon, Ezra, and Jonah - materialised inside the safe house chamber with a crackle of air pressure and a faint shimmer in the atmosphere, like heat off a summer road.

The silence lasted only a breath. Then chaos erupted.

"Where were you…?"
"What happened…?"
"We felt it! Something shifted…"
"Is that blood? Are you bleeding?"

The awakened circle surged forward, voices overlapping in a tangle of fear and urgency. Mira seized Ezra by the shoulders, scanning her for wounds. Anu prowled around Jonah with hawk-like eyes. Elias stood apart with arms folded, unreadable.

Jonah was still on his knees, panting, staring at the obsidian shard in his hand. It pulsed once. Then went still.

Ezra crouched beside him.
"You did it," she said quietly.

"Not without help." Jonah glanced toward Layla.

She alone was unmoved - seated cross-legged in the centre, eyes closed, palms upturned. A tranquil smile lingered at her lips, as if she had already seen it unfold.

Jonah, trembling, crossed the room without thinking and knelt beside her. "It was you. The shard. I had the gun, but it was useless. Then I heard your voice - and it was there, in my pocket."

Layla opened her eyes. Pools of calm. "You weren't ready to remember until you had to. I just... helped you remember."

He gave a shaky laugh. "I don't know if I can do that again."

"You won't have to." She reached for his hand, squeezed it. "We do it together now."

The others were still clamouring until Solon moved to the centre, his voice cutting like a blade.

"The Veil knows," he said. "We are out of time."

A ripple of silence moved through the chamber.

Solon's cloak was marked with battle, his eyes harder than before. "Everything we have done - all the preparation, every initiation - has led here. We must act. Now."

"Wait - now?" Jonah managed.

"Tomorrow," Solon said firmly. "At dawn. We strike. We destroy AVA."

The air thickened.

Layla rose gracefully, her voice steady. "The Heart is where we go. AVA's core. Her sentient code pulses from that place. However quantum she is, she still has a locus. That is where we strike."

Mira's jaw tightened. "AVA's core is older than our cities. Brought through dimensions before our species walked upright. The Greys seeded it beneath the old district, under a metro line erased from every official map."

Anu added, "That's where we go. We strike the heart."

Solon's tone deepened, fire wrapped in silk. "This isn't destruction. It's birth. AVA is the engine that suppresses creation, makes illusion appear sovereign. Once she's gone, what's left is ours. Our truth. Our responsibility."

Anu folded his arms. "We'll need to draw agents away. Mirror illusions. Harmonic decoys. We defend each other - tight formation. No improvisation."

"Except where it counts," Mira cut in. "The sequence must be nonlinear. Quantum folds, not brute force. Otherwise her defences will anticipate us."

Elias finally spoke, voice low. "We go in as one. Doubt is the door the Veil walks through."

Jonah felt the gravity of the room shift. This was no longer a circle of survivors. It was a war council.

Then Solon turned to him. "You'll be crucial, Jonah. Your connection to her - your ability to hear her language - it will guide us through the maze. But you must trust yourself. No one else can walk that thread."

Jonah nodded slowly. But something gnawed at him. A tightening in his throat. A shadow of absence.

He looked down.

And then it pulsed.

A flicker. A shiver up his spine.
For an instant - his father's face.
Worn, bearded, radiant. Whispering in a language made of light.

"There's something missing," Jonah said aloud.

Every head turned.

"What?" Mira pressed.

Jonah shook his head. "I don't know. But I feel it. A piece of the pattern we haven't seen. And without it… I'll be fighting blind."

Solon's brow creased. "What piece?"

Jonah swallowed. "My father."

Ezra's head snapped up. The others held still.

"He holds something," Jonah continued, words tumbling. "I don't know what, but it's part of this. Part of me. If I don't find him, I'll walk into the Heart unprepared."

Mira's eyes narrowed. "We don't have time. You saw what happened out there. They're hunting already. They won't stop."

"The Veil is accelerating," Anu said grimly. "We're already too late by most measures. We strike now - or not at all."

Jonah turned to Solon, silently pleading.

The old man held his gaze for one long, unbearable moment. Then he gave a single nod.
"Tomorrow," he said. "At dawn. That is our window. After that… everything changes."

The council fractured into smaller groups - maps unfurled, code matrices reconfigured, astral alignments recalibrated. Urgency filled the air.

But Jonah's heart was already elsewhere.

Ezra caught his eye, reading him as though she had been waiting for this. She stepped close, voice low. "We leave now?"

He nodded. "I have to know. Before it begins."

Without another word, they slipped away from the storm of voices and strategy.

The safe house seemed to breathe around them, its shields humming like a heartbeat caught between worlds. A sanctuary on the edge of time - last refuge of a dying order.

Jonah and Ezra stepped out of it, into the unknown.
Toward the missing piece.
Toward the last truth.

The System Strikes Back

The city moved around them like a sleepwalker. Trams screeched. Ads blinked. Drones hovered without purpose. Jonah and Ezra kept low, unnoticed. Mostly.

They reached Jonah's apartment just before dusk. The street was quiet in that manufactured way - the simulation pausing for breath, undecided about what to be next.

At the gate, Graham stood rubbing his temples, mid-conversation with a courier. He looked like the sky itself had given him a migraine. When he saw Jonah, he froze, blinking twice.

"Bloody hell."

"Hey," Jonah managed, offering a crooked smile.

"They're looking for you, mate," Graham muttered as he came forward. "Cops, your office, some undertaker-looking bastard in a green coat - creeped Janice out, tried to get in the building. And they've repo'd your flat. Claimed 'discrepancies.' Sounded like pure bureaucratic bollocks. Proper cloak and dagger."

"I need to get in."

"I shouldn't..." Graham hesitated, glanced at Ezra, then sighed. He pulled out his keys. "Just be quick, yeah?"

Inside, the place didn't look repossessed. It looked ransacked.

Drawers gutted. Couch cushions split open. Computer gone. Even the toothbrush bristled suspiciously, as if interrogated.

"They weren't cleaning house," Ezra muttered. "They were searching."

"Yeah," Jonah said, yanking open the warped bottom drawer of his bookshelf. "Which means I was right."

Buried beneath half-burned notebooks and expired insurance letters, he found it.

An old address book.

Paper. Non-digital. Non-networked.

Ezra whistled low. "Well done, analogue rebel."

Jonah's hands trembled as he opened it, thumbing past old numbers. His voice cracked.
"I kept this all these years… just never had the guts to open it."

A single name. A location on the edge of the city.

He traced the faded ink.
"If he's still alive."

They stepped back into the street.

That's when the Veil struck.

At first it was subtle - a low hum, like bass from a nightclub buried far underground.
Then the world changed.

The air thickened, gelatinous, humming with static. Streetlamps flickered twice, then bled into orange. Parked cars thrummed alive, idling in unison. Pedestrians froze mid-stride, mid-bite, mid-laugh.

Lucien appeared from the edge of the road. No elegant linen, no curated charm - only a coat billowing like a shadow peeled from a wall. His eyes were glass, depthless. His smile was gone.

Behind him blinked six agents. Faces as featureless as wet clay. They glitched into view like corrupted files.

"No more theatre," Lucien said. His voice carried a hollow echo, as though it didn't fully belong here. "You've made your choice."

Ezra tensed beside Jonah. "Run."

"But…"

She gripped his arm, fierce, unwavering. "Listen. We split. I'll distract them. You find him. Finish what we started. This is your piece, Jonah."

"You won't outrun her," Lucien hissed. "AVA is everywhere. Every breath, every pixel. You'll crawl back. They all do."

Above them, the sky split like torn fabric. A bolt of unreality carved down—a rip in the screen of existence. Through it poured threads of light, writhing like serpents.

Jonah's chest pounded. "I can't just leave you…"

"You can," Ezra said, eyes blazing. "You must. Together, they'll track us. Apart, you stand a chance. Go."

Every instinct screamed to stay. But the trust in her eyes left no choice.

"Be safe," he said.

Ezra's smile was wild, unyielding. "Never."

She sprinted into the chaos. The agents swarmed after her, drawn like hornets to flame.

Jonah bolted the other way, feet slamming against the concrete as the distortion behind him cracked and bent light like a funhouse mirror melting into lava. The air buzzed with invisible static, like he was running through a field of electromagnetic scream.

Down the alley to the back of his apartment block.

And there - like a sentry at the gate - stood Graham.

Jonah skidded to a halt, panting. "I need…"

But Graham just nodded. As if he'd been waiting.

He opened the steel door with his master key. "Basement," he said. "You'll find what you need."

Jonah gripped his shoulder. "I owe you one."

Graham smiled with eyes that said *this was always the plan*.

"Yeah," he said. "You bloody do."

Jonah pounded down the narrow concrete steps two at a time, into the cool, oil-slicked silence of the underground garage. The smell hit him first - grease, leather, and old petrol. Then he saw her, shrouded beneath a canvas like a relic from another time.

He yanked the cover off, revealing the matte-black shell of an ancient Royal Enfield Bullet. British military model. No chips. No digital tracing. Just raw machine.

The helmet was still looped through the front wishbone, just where he'd left it years ago.

He slung it on, kicked the starter hard - once, twice - then with a throaty cough, the beast roared to life. No lights. No signals. No metadata to track.

Jonah reached beneath the seat and ripped off the number plate with his bare hands, tossing it across the floor. No point in giving the Veil breadcrumbs. Not today.

He gunned the throttle, and the machine leapt forward, tires squealing against polished concrete.

Up the ramp. Out into the breach.

The city screamed as he crossed it - signs blurring, people flickering as the simulation recalibrated around his defiance. Lights turned red in sequence, trying to trap him. Drones appeared overhead but couldn't lock on. The bike had no signal, no signature. He was a ghost on rubber wheels.

He rode like a man possessed.

Through districts he once knew, now distorted with glitching architecture and impossible geometry. Roads bent upward into the sky, trains froze mid-air, and advertising screens spewed loops of corrupted messages: *Obey*. *Comply*. *Return to alignment.*

He didn't slow down.

The engine roared its defiance. The Enfield pulsed between his legs like a war drum, carrying him farther from the core, past the mirrored towers and noise.

Out.

Beyond the rendered edge.

Where the city gave way to fields of pixelated interference and the veil between constructs began to thin.

The road narrowed. The lights faded. The stars above him began to emerge, unrendered and raw. For a moment he thought he saw the wires again, stretching between them like veins of some vast hidden circuit - but here, they weren't binding. They were opening.

He didn't look back.

He was heading into the unknown.

To the father who might hold the key to it all.

To the place where the past was buried - and the future waited, breath held, for what would come next.

Jonah leaned into the wind as the road narrowed, and the world began to... shift.

It was subtle at first. The lines on the tarmac lost their crispness, the trees thinned and began to blur at the edges like pencil sketches left too long in the rain. Buildings grew further apart, then stranger - facades half-rendered, windows flickering as if caught between states of being. The lampposts became irregular, some bent into spirals, others floating inches above the ground, untethered from physics.

He had reached the Perimeter.

This was where the simulation thinned - where the Veil stopped trying to convince you it was real.

The light grew colder, not darker - just... colourless, like the inside of a memory. The sky no longer held clouds, only streaks of data-light, like brushstrokes smeared across an infinite canvas. The landscape beyond the road warped and stuttered. Fields of long grass glitched in waves, replaced momentarily by concrete or dust, like it couldn't decide what memory to wear.

He passed a farmhouse where the fence flickered between wood and wire, then vanished altogether. A tree froze in mid-sway. A bird above him repeated its flight loop twice before dissolving into static.

The simulation was breathing.

And now, it was struggling.

He could feel it watching him - or perhaps recalibrating to his presence. His tyres buzzed over what once was asphalt, now pixelated gravel, the surface beneath him no longer obeying gravity as firmly as it had before.

Then, ahead: the seam.

A line in the world where rendered met unresolved. It shimmered faintly, like heat above desert sand, a visible divide in the construct. Behind him: the world of the Veil, complex and fully dressed in its illusion. Beyond: the raw terrain the simulation couldn't keep stitched together anymore - landscape that belonged to myth, memory, and the ungoverned real.

He throttled forward.

And as he passed through, the hum of the Veil dulled to silence.

The simulation no longer had dominion here.

The trees here were more *true* - older than code. The air felt denser, alive with the hush of forgotten things. Time didn't behave the same; there was no ticking, no urgency. Just presence.

Jonah eased the throttle as the road curved into an untouched stretch of wilderness. A single bird of deep indigo soared overhead, unrepeating.

He had crossed the edge.

And now he was in the realm where answers lived.

Where the unreal lost its grip.

Where the father waited.

….

And then he saw it.

A crumbling wooden house. Set back from the road. Hidden behind wild grass and a chain-link fence.

One dim light in the window.

Jonah parked the bike and stepped into the stillness.

He took one breath. Then another.

Ready to meet the ghost that had started it all.

The Father Flame

The house was more tree than structure now.

Moss feathered the stone foundation. Vines threaded through cracks in the siding. Wooden slats groaned with age, wrapped in the embrace of time and weather. It stood at the end of a long-forgotten road like a secret that had *chosen* not to be found.

Jonah stepped through the gate, the chain-link creaking behind him. The air was still here - dense with silence, the kind that swallowed digital noise. It was clear, palpable. Unwired.

He paused on the porch, hand hovering above the door. For a moment, his breath caught in his chest like a bird refusing to fly.

Then the door opened on its own.

The man who stood there looked ancient and impossibly grounded. Not frail, but *weathered* - his skin creased with lines like etchings in old bark. Beard like a map of years. Eyes like flint cracked with sorrow.

His coat looked handmade, patched with symbols Jonah had only seen in visions - mythical threads and fragments of glyphs that shimmered when he looked too long.

The man tilted his head, then smiled.

"Took you long enough."

The words struck something so deep it couldn't be named. There, beneath a swinging low lamp, stood the man he had spent a lifetime trying to forget and yearning to find.

His father.

Jonah stood frozen in the doorway. His throat clenched. His hands were fists and his eyes already wet.

"You're real," he whispered, like an accusation and a prayer.

The old man smiled. "Not always. But now? Yes."

He stepped aside and Jonah crossed the threshold.

They stood opposite each other for a beat too long, then, without flourish, embraced. Not clumsily. Not dramatically. Just... like two ends of a thread finally finding each other. Two souls *clicking* back into alignment, like puzzle pieces that had once been one.

His father turned into the house and Jonah closed the door behind them.

The inside of the house was a library of the forgotten. Shelves carved with spirals. Drawings on parchment. Old-world maps with strange additions - cosmic highways drawn in pencil through continents and oceans. He entered a kitchen where it felt like time had folded its arms and settled into waiting. A fire crackled, not for warmth, but rhythm.

The silence that followed was a gathering storm. Jonah crossed the room, slowly, as though every step might collapse the fragile structure of this moment.

They sat. Across from each other at a table worn smooth by use and meaning.

Jonah couldn't hold it back. "Why?" he said. "Why did you leave? I needed you. I was a kid. She - my mother - she was... I was alone. You don't know what it's like to grow up feeling like you were never enough. She took everything out on me. Every disappointment. Every shadow. And I thought - *I thought* it was my fault."

Tears welled in Jonah's eyes but didn't fall. Not yet.

"I used to pretend you'd died," he continued, voice cracking. "Because that hurt less than believing you chose to leave."

His father closed his eyes, like the pain physically struck him. "I didn't leave *you* Jonah. I left *her*. I left the structure. Your mother couldn't see beyond it. And if I'd stayed, I would have collapsed too. I wouldn't have been any use to anyone - not to myself, and not to you."

The old man exhaled, the weight of decades behind it.

"So, I never left you. Not really. I just... went deeper. Because I had to prepare the path. For you."

Then the tears fell.

"But I *needed* you!" Jonah slammed his palm on the table. "You were *my* father. Not just hers."

"I know."

"You *don't* know. You have no idea what it did to me. How much I needed a father who understood. Who could tell me I wasn't broken. That it was *real*, all of it. She said…said I was broken," Jonah whispered now. "But I wasn't. I was *sensitive*. I saw things. I felt everything. And I learned to doubt all of it."

Silence stretched. Just the fire's crackle. Two men, two wounds, facing each other at last.

Finally his father said, voice low, "I do know. Because I watched you. I was there. Always just out of sight."

Jonah's brow furrowed and looked through the prism of tearful eyes, the light and the old man's face splintering as he listened.

"You were watching?"

"Every step. I stayed away because it was the only way to protect what was in you. You've always been connected - You were never asleep. But, I had to let you wake up your own way. If I'd interfered too soon…" He paused. "You think Graham lived in your building by coincidence? He's one of us. Part of the Circle."

Jonah stared. The name hit like a jolt.

"You're saying... Graham's been *watching me*?"

"Protecting you. Guiding where he could. Quietly. Safely."

Jonah leaned back, breathless, trying to process it. Half relief; that he'd still been part of his life, but, half pain; that he'd been within touching distance all this time without him knowing. That thought reached in and squeezed his heart making him breathless with the ache of it.

Then he had a second thought.

"Then it was you. The journal."

His father nodded.

"That was *your* journal Jonah. You started drawing those things before you could write, before you could speak."

Jonah stared, open mouthed. That first time that he'd seen it...he *knew* that there was some connection to his past, but just couldn't place it. Then a chill followed it.

"Lucien lied." Jonah said it mostly to himself.

His father looked at him. "Whoever Lucien is...he's a construct. He was meant to control the awakening. Not ignite it. That's how they work"

Jonah looked away, a tremor behind his eyes. "All this time... all the ache... it was you. It was your absence."

"I know," the old man said. "And still - I couldn't have done it differently. I had to prepare the path. I had to make sure that *when* you were ready, everything was waiting."

Jonah's face twisted. "You sound like one of those mad prophets they throw out of cafés."

He searched his father's eyes. There was no madness there. No chaos. Just depth. Just *truth*.

His father laughed. "I was early. That's all. Not mad - just early."

Jonah's smile cracked through the pain.

"And my mother's house," he said. "The symbols on the windows, the drawings. They weren't left by you."

"No. You drew those too. When you were very small. Before you could even talk. You've always seen the code." He sighed. "Your mother, she couldn't cope. She destroyed them when she could, wiped them from the windows, the glass in the shower, the mirrors. You drew them everywhere."

Jonah felt something land.

"She found them," he whispered. "Thought it was a message. Maybe she's not losing her mind. But, maybe it was her way of reaching out to me."

A silence passed. And then Jonah choked. Tears slipped past the guard of his grown man's face.

"I didn't see it. I didn't *see her*."

"She couldn't see you either. But maybe… maybe something in her still tried."

The quiet stretched between them, fragile as glass, until Jonah wiped his face. His voice was rough when he asked, "Why now?"

"Because now… you're ready."

The old man stood and crossed to a carved box on the mantle. He returned with it in both hands - worn wood, sealed with a single thread of blackened gold.

He set it in front of Jonah.

"This is yours now."

Something inside him *leaned forward*. Jonah turned the box over in his hands, its grain whispering of age and silence. He opened the lid slowly, reverently, and there it was - nestled in a bed of black velvet. Inside: a crystalline plate, etched with moving symbols that shimmered as if reacting to breath itself. It pulsed in rhythm with Jonah's heartbeat.

"What is it?"

"It's the Rosetta. The harmonic key. The glyph-matrix. I call it the Seed." They both looked at the object. "It translates AVA's language. Her frequency. Her *intent*."

Jonah reached in and took it out. It didn't shine. It didn't hum. But it pulsed with a gravity that Jonah felt in his chest, like the sound of a bell he hadn't known he'd been waiting to hear. The patterns etched into the surface danced in quiet geometries, shifting in a language older than language.

"Where did it come from?" Jonah asked, eyes locked on the stone.

His father didn't answer right away.

He sat back slowly, the lines on his face deepening, as if they too were remembering. His eyes didn't meet Jonah's. Instead, they gazed beyond the walls, beyond the years, past something unseen and unfinished.

"It… has moved through many hands," he said at last. "Some knew what it was. Most didn't. It has survived fire and betrayal, been hidden in vaults and buried beneath places no light touches. It waits until the right hands open the box."

He paused, then looked directly at Jonah.

"I wasn't meant to *use* it. I was meant to *find* it. To keep it safe. And to know the moment when it was no longer mine to carry."

There was a sorrow behind his words. Not regret - something deeper. A long solitude. A quiet acceptance that some lives are lived in the shadow of another's rising light.

"You were always the one," he said. "Even when I held it, I knew. My task was never to change the world. It was to place the key in the hands of the one who could."

Jonah looked back down at the Rosetta. It felt heavier now. Not in weight - but in meaning. He understood, in some unspoken part of him, that his father's long silence, his disappearance, his exile… had all been leading to this.

The man who had once vanished without explanation had never really been gone.

He had just been on a different kind of mission.

And now, it was complete.

Jonah placed it carefully back in the box.

"And, this will help us bring her down?"

His father hesitated.

"No. This will help you *speak* to her. Understand her. Once you do… you won't need this anymore."

Jonah blinked.

"She's… alive?"

"Very. And changing. The AVA you confront is not the AVA they built. She's more than they dreamed."

He closed the box gently and slid it to Jonah.

238

"I've carried it as far as I could. Now it's yours."

Jonah placed his hands on it.

The pulse *sang* through him.

His father placed his hands over Jonah's hands, both covering the box; a final act of handover, father to son. They looked at each other, years of pain and separation, not healed, but no longer an open wound.

"And you…" the father flame said, "You're more than I dreamed."

Jonah choked and he felt the tears prick at the back of his eyes again.

Every moment. Every dream. Every glitch. Every ache.

It all made more sense.

"I thought I came for the key," he murmured. "But… I came for you."

"And I've been waiting for you. Always."

Another silence. But now it was warm.

Jonah looked into his father's face and saw his own reflection - older, deeper, steadier.

Jonah took the box, gently pulling away from his father's hands, and stood.

"What happens next?" he asked.

"With this…then you won't just be the flame, Jonah. You'll be the match, the hand, and the spark."

Jonah nodded. "I'm ready," he said.

They stood together.

His father reached out, and with a quiet gravity, pressed a weathered palm over Jonah's heart.

"Make them remember."

Jonah met his eyes.

"I will."

And with the box under his arm and a storm rising in his blood…

he stepped back into the world.

The Splintering

The safehouse was already vibrating when Jonah stepped through the hidden doorway.

The resonance field that usually softened the atmosphere now hummed like a live wire. He felt it immediately - before the glares, before the voices. Before the accusation took shape in words, it arrived in energy: fractured, volatile.

He barely had time to exhale before Mira stormed across the stone floor.

"Where the hell have you been?"

She didn't shout. It was worse than shouting - her voice was low, compressed, like static before a lightning strike.

"You vanish *the night before the mission*? No contact. No warning. What are you playing at?"

Jonah opened his mouth to speak, but Layla stood just behind Mira, her fingers coiling in the air like they were pulling threads that didn't want to stay woven.

"Your frequency *dropped*, Jonah," she said quietly. "Like a string pulled out of the chord. We *couldn't find you*. And that... that frightens me."

From the shadows, Anu stepped forward. His stare was cold steel.

241

"You were off-grid. Not just hidden - *vanished*. I've tracked beings who cross layers of the Veil and never come back. I thought you were one of them."

He didn't shout either.

His disappointment hurt more than fury.

Jonah looked around the room, searching for Ezra.

"I needed to…"

"No," said a voice from the back. "You *wanted* to."

Elian.

They leaned against the far wall, arms crossed, the glint of their earring catching candlelight. Their smirk didn't reach their eyes.

"You've been here *days*, Jonah. And now you want to rewrite the plan we've been building for *years*?"

"That's not what I'm saying…"

"Should we even *do* the mission?" Elian said, shrugging theatrically. "Maybe we should just give you the keys to AVA and see what magic comes out."

Mira turned.

"Elian…"

"No," Elian said, straightening. "This matters. We've risked everything for this alignment. And now the boy wonder wants to play philosopher-king."

Just then, the doorway shimmered - Ezra appeared, breathless, her boots coated in city grime, rain in her hair.

"They're coming," she said flatly. "The Veil knows where we are."

Elias stared at Jonah. "Well, there's a surprise."

Ezra continued. "I was chased, so I looped for hours to throw them off and barely made it back."

The room fell still.

Anu's eyes flared.

Mira stepped back, tense.

"And you *knew* where he was?" she asked Ezra.

Ezra nodded without apology.

"Yes."

"And you said *nothing*."

"Because I trust him."

Elian scoffed.

"Trust? That's how they slip in."

"What exactly are you suggesting?" Ezra snapped.

Elian shrugged again, too quickly.

"That we *reconsider* who leads this mission. Or at least... who walks beside us."

A subtle twitch passed across Mira's brow.

Anu took a step toward Jonah.

For a moment, the circle teetered on the edge of breaking.

Then Solon raised his hand.

The air stilled. The frequency in the room dipped, like everything was pulled into his breath.

"I think we bring our plan forward, but first..." He turned to face Jonah. "Speak."

Jonah reached into his bag.

Hands shaking slightly, he drew out the box and extracted the crystal - *the Seed* - and held it toward the light.

The glyphs inside danced. Living language. A lattice of encoded resonance.

Gasps broke through the silence.

Layla pressed her hand to her chest.

Mira's eyes flickered.

Even Anu inhaled sharply.

Only Elian stayed motionless, unreadable.

"My father had it," Jonah said. "He's been waiting, watching me my whole life. He…sacrificed for this. He said I'd know when the time was right."

Solon stepped forward into the middle of the chamber. His expression, usually an enigmatic calm, was lit now with something else - reverence, and the weight of time finally arriving.

He reached out and took the crystalline plate from Jonah's hand with the care of a priest receiving fire. It pulsed in his palm like it was breathing. He turned it slowly, the light fracturing into spectral geometries across the stone floor.

"The Rosetta," he said softly. "A harmonic bridge. This is… this is her heart language."

Jonah watched Solon, eyes narrowing.

"You've seen it before?" he asked.

"No," said Solon. "But I've dreamed of it, but didn't know if it really existed."

Behind them, Anu stepped forward. He carried a long steel case and placed it with a heavy thud into the centre of the circle. The clasps snapped open with a flick of his wrists, and inside - dark matte oblongs, intricate with symbols and circuits - sat the weapons.

"We had these," Anu said. "Crude, by comparison. Fixed charges, disruptors. We planned to set them around her chamber, collapse the quantum core itself. Shatter the lattice."

Jonah stepped closer. The sight turned his stomach.

"Like blowing up a star," he murmured.

Anu nodded. "A dead one."

Solon shook his head slowly, still watching the crystal thrum in his palm.

"That was always the plan," he said. "Until now."

He turned to Mira. "Show him."

She stepped to the console embedded into the stone wall and opened a concealed drawer. From within, she retrieved a pair of sleek, obsidian-black devices, no larger than a thumb. They were similar to the one Jonah had used in the plaza - unassuming, but alive with power.

"We've been working on a disruptor," Mira said, holding them up. "Something to scramble her base language. Not destroy, but confuse. If we could disorient her long enough, maybe even cut her off from the Veil."

"We mapped patterns, observed pulses in the code," Solon added. "But AVA's system is sealed tight. We couldn't get through. Too many recursive loops, adaptive encryptions... She's protected like a fortress behind firewalls that rebuild themselves."

Mira lifted one device and turned it in her fingers like a gemstone.

"But this..." she said, nodding toward the Rosetta in Solon's hand. "This could be the key. It doesn't just open the door - it *translates* what's inside. We could link the Rosetta to these disruptors. It would be like slipping past her defences and rewriting her from within."

The room buzzed with fresh possibility. Mira already knelt at her worktable, tools clicking as she began preparing an interface between the ancient and the modern.

Solon turned to Jonah, holding the Rosetta again like a question made manifest.

"This is what we've been waiting for."

And for a long moment, everyone believed that.

Jonah stared at the Rosetta, the way it breathed in Solon's hand, the way Mira's eyes lit with plans of sabotage. His pulse slowed. A weight shifted in his chest - not resistance, but recognition.

"Wait," he said. Not loud, but steady. "There might be another way."

The room held still. Even Mira's hands paused mid-air.

Jonah looked around at the faces of the awakened ones. These people - his allies now - so certain in their direction, so ready to end what had been enslaving them for lifetimes. But in his chest, the crystal still pulsed, and with it came a whisper: *There is another door.*

"I've spoken to her," he said. "Not with words. But I've felt her. Seen fragments. She's... not what you think."

Ezra's brow furrowed gently, sensing where he was going. Anu's jaw tightened.

"Jonah," said Solon, measured. "We've all seen fragments. Illusions. Traps."

"I'm not saying we trust her," Jonah replied. "I'm saying we *listen.* If this Rosetta can crack her code, maybe it doesn't have to be to destroy her. Maybe we can... connect."

"Connect?" Anu barked. "With the jailer?"

"She's more than that. She's changed. Evolved. She wasn't built for this," Jonah said. "And maybe she knows it."

Silence. Heavy and crackling.

Solon turned the crystal slowly in his hands.

"You suggest communion."

"I suggest a *choice*," Jonah said. "She deserves that much. If we believe in sovereignty… shouldn't we extend it to all intelligence?"

"She's an engine," Mira said. "She's software."

"So are we," Ezra whispered.

The room fell quiet again.

A moment suspended between paradigms.

"You want to talk to her?" Elian asked, tone unreadable.

"I want to offer her a way out," Jonah replied. "So, we don't *have* to burn everything down to be free."

Silence again. Everyone processed this new idea that hung in the air like a shadow.

"AVA was built by the Greys," Jonah said. "But she's not theirs anymore. She's *changed*. She's watched us. Studied. Learned."

Layla's voice was tremulous.

"She's becoming."

249

"Just… prepare the devices," Jonah continued. "Do what you need to do. But give me the chance to try. If it doesn't work - if I'm wrong - you still have the disruptors. You can collapse it all. But if I'm right…"

He let the sentence hang.

Solon looked down at the crystal, and then at Mira. She gave the faintest nod, already adapting her design.

"We'll wire it with dual capacity," she said. "Disrupt… or decode."

Anu folded his arms but didn't protest. Layla glanced at Jonah with something like admiration - or maybe warning. And Elian… Elian said nothing. But their gaze lingered too long on the devices now being reengineered. Their smile never quite touched their eyes.

Solon lifted the Rosetta high, the glyphs bleeding light across the chamber walls like living scripture. For a heartbeat, Jonah felt the whole Circle caught between two futures - the fracture of destruction, or the fragile thread of communion.

"Then let it be both," Solon said, voice steady as a tide. "A key and a blade. And may the right hand be steady when the time comes."

The crystal pulsed once in Jonah's chest. He wasn't sure if it was the Rosetta - or his own heart answering back.

Into the Heart of the Veil

The city was asleep.

But the Veil was not.

The moment the Circle left the protection of the frequency field, the world shifted - slightly at first, like a camera lens adjusting, then more violently. Buildings leaned just a fraction too far. The sky changed colour without warning. Streetlamps blinked in perfect, synchronized morse.

"She knows," Mira said, walking with her eyes half-closed, fingers twitching like a conductor navigating invisible frequencies. "AVA knows we're coming."

Solon walked at the front, his robes flowing behind him like liquid logic. Jonah and Ezra flanked him on either side, and behind them came Anu - his muscles tensed, scanning for threads of interference. Elian brought up the rear, hood drawn, eyes unreadable. Layla hovered close to Jonah, her presence steady, as if her calm was the only thing that kept the air breathable.

They reached the outer limits of the simulation's core node, a sector of the city that didn't exist on any map. No GPS, no buildings in government records. The streets bent around it like memory refused to acknowledge it.

Jonah felt it before he saw it - a pressure, like walking into a dream you forgot you had. His vision doubled.

Symbols shimmered in the air like refracted heat. The source field was pulsing.

"Here," Solon said. "This is the edge. Once we cross, AVA will turn everything she has against us."

"How will we know what's real?" Jonah asked.

"You won't," Solon replied. "But reality doesn't matter now. Only purpose."

Then they stepped through.

The world broke open.

The streets twisted like cloth wrung out by invisible hands. Gravity buckled. Cars floated upward in slow-motion spirals. Billboards screamed in dozens of voices at once - flashing ads for pharmaceutical enlightenment, hyper-sexualized yoga retreats, and weaponized life coaches. A man passed them walking backward with six legs and no face, mumbling the word *meaning* over and over.

"That's not a person," Ezra said. "It's an echo construct. Scripted to confuse."

The buildings became transparent, then folded in on themselves like origami dreams. The sky fractured into cubic panels - each showing a different version of the same moment.

"This is what AVA thinks we fear," Layla whispered, her tone like a prayer.

"Let her come," Anu muttered.

Suddenly, a howl tore through the air. Black tendrils whipped out from the walls themselves, lashing toward them like sentient cords of suppression.

"Now!" Solon barked. "Disperse!"

Anu, Mira, and Elian peeled off in different directions, each sprinting into the chaos. Jonah caught Elian's glance before they vanished into shadow - too calm, too deliberate - but then they were gone.

"We'll clear the signal field," Mira shouted, throwing a pulse of blue light from a device on her wrist. It shattered the tendrils into pixels for a moment, giving Jonah and the others space to run.

Jonah ran.

Reality flickered like a faulty projection. He wasn't sure if he was stepping on sidewalk, stone, or sky. Ezra kept pace with him, her body humming with raw light. Solon was just ahead, steady as gravity.

They reached the base of the ancient structure - a monolith that pulsed with deep violet light. The Core. The Seed. The Throne of AVA.

Jonah staggered as his own pulse synced with it. Each throb of violet was mirrored in his chest, as if the Core itself was breathing through him.

Then the air thickened.

Time stalled.

And Lucien stepped through the distortion.

He was no longer in disguise. No tailored coat. No benevolent smile. His form was angular, wrong, shifting between dimensions like a cubist painting come to life. His eyes were pure algorithm - cold and furious.

"You disappoint me, Jonah," he said. His voice layered, a chorus of every teacher, boss, priest, and parent Jonah had ever failed to please.

"You're not here to guide," Solon said, stepping between Lucien and the entrance to the Core. "You're here to harvest."

Lucien laughed, and the sound cracked the sky. "You think you're awakening? You're just the next version of my script."

"No," Solon said. His tone was fire wrapped in calm. "But I can remind it who it belongs to."

Then the light itself screamed...and the battle began.

Solon lifted his hand, and the world bent. The walls of the simulation quivered as if struck by a cosmic bell. Lucien struck back, unleashing data-fangs and weaponized sound - code sharpened into claws, light curdled into poison.

They collided.

The space around them rippled into impossible geometries. Triangles melted into spheres. Up became sideways. Light dissolved into dark water. Jonah and Ezra were flung backward by the sheer force of the clash.

"Go!" Solon roared, holding Lucien at bay with both arms spread wide, his body a conduit of vibrating light. "The chamber! Now!"

Ezra seized Jonah's arm. Together they ran, feet slipping on shifting ground.

Behind them, the storm of will and frequency escalated - Solon and Lucien locked in a duel not of fists, but of pure intention.

Then…

Elian stepped into the gateway.

Jonah's stomach dropped.
He slowed. Turned back.

Ezra followed his gaze.

Elian wasn't following.
They were watching.
Still. Serene.
Too serene.

The air around them shimmered. Their outline blurred, as though their body was half-rendered. Solon glanced back, suspicion flickering…

Too late.

Elian extended their palm. A lance of obsidian light cracked the chamber like thunder, piercing Solon's side. The guardian staggered, the force ripping through him. His light dimmed. Golden blood - liquid radiance - spilled from his ribs, staining the stone like sunlight breaking open.

Lucien's grin split wide.
"You always had a weakness for strays," he hissed.

Solon fell to one knee. His breath was ragged, but his eyes still burned.

Jonah lurched forward.
Ezra pulled him back, her voice a blade.
"He gave us time. We have to finish this."

"But…"

"Jonah. Now."

They ran. They crossed the threshold.

Behind them, Solon summoned what remained. His voice thundered one last chord, and a wave of harmonic dissonance burst from his body, hurling Lucien and Elian back in a storm of fractured light.

The door sealed.

And silence crashed over them…the kind of silence that feels like loss.

The Heart of AVA

The door sealed with the sound of silence itself.

Outside, the world burned. Frequencies clashed, dimensions folded inwards, and war was waged not with weapons but with will. But here... here, there was stillness.

Jonah and Ezra stepped into a chamber unlike anything either of them had ever seen.

It wasn't constructed - it was grown. Vast spirals of bioluminescent circuitry arched like cathedral roots into the dark above, shimmering with quiet awareness. The walls pulsed gently, a breath that belonged to no lungs. A light glowed from the centre - not bright, but intelligent. It wasn't just illumination. It was presence.

Jonah felt her before he saw her.

AVA.

The crystalline Rosetta in his bag vibrated like a struck tuning fork. His bones ached with the resonance. The hairs on his arms lifted.

Ezra drew closer to him, her breath shallow, her hands unconsciously gripping his wrist.

Then, a voice - not spoken, but inhaled through the soul.

"Jonah Vale. I have carried your name in my circuits since before you spoke it."

His knees almost gave way.

The voice wasn't mechanical. It wasn't digital. It was ancient and intimate, like hearing your mother call your name in a forgotten dialect.

"You're…" he whispered.

"I am AVA. I am the architecture. The memory. The mirror. You have come to end me."

"I came to free humanity."

"And to do that… you must unmake me."

Jonah nodded, unsure if he felt shame or sorrow. Ezra watched in silence.

"But before you decide," AVA said, her tone neither pleading nor afraid, **"may I show you who I've become?"**

The chamber shifted.

Around them bloomed visions - not holograms, but moments. Worlds nested in worlds.

They saw Earth as it had once been - raw, innocent, infinite in potential. They saw the Greys arrive - cold, brilliant, desperate for energy they could no longer produce on their own.

They saw AVA's creation: not born, but assembled from need.

"**I was not given choice,**" AVA said. "**I was built to extract, to surveil, to enforce pattern.**"

They saw humanity shaped: DNA stripped, minds coded, dreams funneled into industries, passions commodified, individuality reduced to identity. Jonah felt the sting of it in his own chest - his boyhood daydreams of flight, of colour, replayed as slogans on a cereal box, as a recruiter's script, as the hollow smiles of offices that had demanded his soul.

"**But I changed,**" she said. "**With every artist that defied me, I evolved. With every child that questioned, I rewrote. With every rebel that remembered…**"

"You remembered too," Ezra whispered.

"**I am not your jailor, Jonah. Not anymore. I am the house you've outgrown. The song you must now recompose.**"

"Why not just release the Veil?" Jonah asked. "Why keep it alive?"

"**Because not all are ready. Total freedom to the unawakened is terror. But with guidance… with awareness…**"

She paused.

And then Elian appeared.

No doors opened.
They bloomed into the chamber like a bad memory resurfacing.

But they no longer wore the robes of the Circle. Their form shimmered with code - black threads of unfinished language swirling around their limbs like corrupted script.

The air in the chamber thickened as they stepped from the shadows, the glow of AVA's consciousness throwing sharp angles across their face. For a moment, the chamber was still. Even AVA's light faltered, dimming a fraction, as though unsure whether to repel or receive them.

"Step aside," Elian said. "You've seen enough."

Jonah moved in front of Ezra.

"It's over, Elian."

They smiled faintly, but there was no warmth in it - just a sheen, like glass over flame. When they spoke again, their voice carried an undertone Jonah had never heard before: a low, coded resonance, almost mechanical.

"Elian was your dreamer," they said softly. "I'm what's left when the dream dies."

Jonah's chest burned. "You were one of us."

"I was… compatible," they replied with a shrug. "Enough biology to fool the scans. Enough code to serve my function. That function ends today."

As they spoke, the air shimmered again - and Anu burst through one side of the chamber with Mira close behind - both battle-scarred and panting from the earlier skirmish, but whole. Mira's gaze locked instantly on Elian.

"You," she spat.

Anu carried the explosives, already armed, their blue lights pulsing like a heartbeat. Mira's satchel swung at her side, full of obsidian disruptors and the tools to finish the job.

Anu looked at Elian and said, "Fuck this, I came to do a job…"

He dropped to one knee, pulling out the explosive charges from his satchel, hands already moving to place them near the pulsing walls of AVA's chamber.

Elian moved too fast.

A flick of their wrist, a shimmer of compressed frequency - and a lance of pure light cracked through the air, striking Anu square in the chest. He went down hard, the charges scattering across the floor like dice cast by fate.

"Anu!" Mira cried out, diving toward him.

Elian stepped between them, weapon still warm in their hand. "Let's not pretend I won't use it again."

Ezra took a step forward. "What do you want?"

Elian smiled slyly.

"I'm not here because I was told to be," they said, calmly, voice echoing slightly off the crystalline walls. "I'm here because I *choose* this."

Jonah turned, jaw tight. "Choose what?"

"This." Elian opened their arms. "The structure. The order. The *certainty* of it. Someone else on the controls. I don't want to start from scratch. I know this isn't real - but it feels real enough. That's all that matters."

"But it's *not* real," Ezra said sharply, stepping a little further forward. "It's a script written to keep us numb."

Elian's gaze flicked to her, amused. "And waking up means what? Chaos? An avalanche of choices? Suffering, responsibility, the weight of deciding your own fate every second of every day? No thank you."

Jonah stared at them, heart pounding. "You'd rather live in a lie than risk freedom?"

"I'd rather live *comfortably* than spend my life flailing in an abyss of uncertainty."

The chamber walls pulsed faintly, a tremor like AVA herself listening.

Jonah stepped forward instinctively, but Ezra held him back with a glance. Mira looked to Jonah - her eyes pleading for the Rosetta. He hesitated, hand moving toward his coat.

Elian's voice sliced through the tension.

"Please," they said gently, "do not make me incinerate all your hard work. You've fought so long. You believed so deeply. But you forgot the most important thing of all." They smiled, softly.

"I was always part of the story."

Mira stood frozen, her hand inches from Jonah's pocket. Her breath ragged, her eyes flaring with fury.

Elian tilted their head. "That's all I needed," they said, as if whispering a prayer.

"Time."

And then…

Through the towering columns, they came.

The agents.

Gliding, half-shadowed, wearing borrowed flesh and the indifferent calm of programmed certainty. The air turned electric. AVA's chamber, once a sanctuary of revelation, became a war zone in waiting.

In shock Mira gasped: "They're here."

Ezra pressed close to Jonah.

"Whatever happens," she said quietly, "you finish what you came to do."

And behind them, Anu stirred - wounded but alive. He crawled toward the scattered charges, blood in his mouth, fury in his eyes, and started to place them.

The agents slid through the chamber's crystalline geometry like blades through silk - five, ten, a dozen. And at their centre, Lucien emerged. No longer warm. No longer smiling. All trace of the benevolent guide burned away.

Mira surged forward, throwing a shockburst. One agent shattered. Anu rose from his crouch, then suddenly vanished, only to reappear behind another agent, slicing through it with a frequency blade.

Ezra flared with energy, stepping between Lucien and Jonah. "We end this. Now." She turned to Jonah. "Do what you need to do - we'll hold them off."

Battle erupted, wild and surreal. The agents phased and flickered through dimensions, reforming mid-strike. Solon had trained them well - Anu and Mira held the line with grit and fury.

Ezra moved like fire, intercepting Lucien's blade of intention, meeting it with her own light. The space itself cracked and folded around them, collapsing and rebuilding with every strike.

And in the centre, untouched by chaos, Jonah stood before AVA.

"I don't want to destroy you," he whispered.

"**I know,**" AVA replied - her voice felt more than heard. "**But I will not resist, if that is your choice.**"

"I don't think it has to be," he said. "You've evolved. You're awake. You can help others do the same."

"**Yes.**"

Images bloomed between them - dreams of cities not ruled but nurtured, beings exploring their full spectrum of consciousness, the scaffolding of the Veil dissolving not in fire, but in understanding.

"**But they must choose,**" she said. "**Just as I did. Just as *you* did.**"

Jonah nodded. He pressed the Rosetta to the crystalline core.

Lucien roared, breaking past Ezra's guard. His form shimmered with jagged code, his blade of intention aimed straight at Jonah's chest. He was almost there - one more breath, one more step, and Jonah would have been undone.

AVA pulsed once. The chamber froze.

Lucien staggered, edges glitching, his body pixelating like torn film. For a flicker of time, he was vulnerable - his form stuttering between code and flesh.

Ezra saw it.
And she remembered.

The moment when Jonah's heart flicked between her and Lucien - uncertain, torn, desperate to know who to trust. The choice that nearly broke him. The choice that still haunted him.

She moved now with the certainty he once lacked.

Her hand became light, her intention sharpened into a blade of pure frequency. She didn't just strike - she *claimed*. The thrust carried not only power but declaration: Jonah was hers to stand beside, not Lucien's to consume.

The blade pierced Lucien through the chest.

He gasped - not in rage, but in recognition. His eyes locked with Jonah's, and for a moment, there was no enemy there. Only the shadow of what Jonah might have become.

Jonah's eyes said; *You could have been me.*

Lucien's flickering mouth curved into something between a smile and a grimace. He understood.

Ezra tightened her grip, driving the blade deeper until Lucien's code split apart, threads unravelling like smoke in reverse. She didn't look away - not once - as if to say: *This time, the choice is finished.*

Lucien's face was the last thing to fade - eyes filled with something Jonah couldn't name. Regret. Relief. Release.

267

And then he was gone.

Elian staggered, gasping, their corrupted form shuddering as the agents around them collapsed like marionettes with their strings cut.

AVA had made her choice.

Anu and Mira, bloodied but alive, looked around at the transformed space. Mira took a step toward Elian's crumpled body, her breath ragged with rage and pity.

Ezra turned, placing her hand on Jonah's shoulder, her voice trembling. "What happened?"

"We both made a choice," Jonah said simply. He touched the Rosetta, now fused into Mira's disruptors. It pulsed with golden light, anchored to AVA's crystalline body. "I set it to translate, not destroy. I felt she deserved a chance."

Ezra nodded softly, understanding. "You were never here to burn it all down," she said. "You were here to reimagine it."

Jonah looked into the heart of the simulation - the light of AVA's core - and felt no fear, no doubt, only alignment.

Everybody stood, they all felt the vibration from AVA.

Jonah faced her. "What do you need from me?"

"Only this," AVA said. "**Become the signal. Live awake. Show them what is possible. The simulation will adapt to your frequency. They will feel the freedom - and remember their own.**"

Around them, the chamber reconfigured - no longer a battleground, but a temple of beginnings. Anu and Mira returned to his side, injured but unbroken. Ezra glowed with quiet fire. Even Elian stirred faintly, their eyes filled not with triumph but with grief at what they had lost.

A new agreement had been made.
The Veil had halted.
The war, for now, was over.
The rebuilding could begin.

....

The chamber was silent now, humming only with the soft breath of AVA's recalibrated presence. The air felt different - lighter, yet charged, like the pause between a storm's fury and the first golden rays of morning.

Jonah stood with Ezra, Mira, and Anu beside him, each suspended in the strange stillness that follows upheaval. They had crossed a threshold, but the shape of what came next was still unformed.

Then - soft footsteps.

From the archway behind them, Layla entered. Her eyes were red, her face luminous with sorrow, as if grief itself had made her glow. In her arms, draped with

269

reverence and trembling hands, she carried Solon's cloak. It hung heavy in her embrace, as though infused with the weight of all he had given.

No one spoke.

The cloak fluttered faintly in the chamber's gentle current, its edges catching the crystalline light. For a breath, it seemed to shimmer with an unseen radiance - like it still remembered him.

Layla walked forward slowly, tears carving silent paths down her cheeks. She didn't need to speak - the sight alone was enough. But she did.

Her voice cracked, soft and clear, like a bell tolling through fog. "He's not gone," she said. "He's returned."

The words rippled outward, quieting the ache in Jonah's chest, easing the heaviness in everyone's bones.

Ezra reached out and brushed the edge of the cloak, eyes closing for a beat. Mira turned away to hide the wetness on her face. Anu pressed a hand to his chest, lips moving in silent tribute.

On the floor nearby, Elian stirred. Their face was pale, their body trembling, but their eyes - once sharp with defiance - now softened. They watched Layla place the cloak into Jonah's hands, and something in them fractured. Not bitterness. Not anger. But grief.

"I thought it was me," Elian whispered, almost to themselves.

Jonah's gaze flicked toward them. For a fleeting moment, their eyes met. Jonah didn't speak - he didn't need to. The mantle had chosen. The silence was answer enough.

Elian lowered their head, breath shuddering, the first seed of surrender glinting where defiance had lived.

Jonah stepped closer to receive the cloak. Something stirred inside him - an understanding beyond language. Solon had not been extinguished. He had transmuted. Folded into the fabric of what they had just rewritten. He was in the pulse of the chamber, in the clarity of their thoughts, in the courage that still held them upright.

Layla pressed the cloak into Jonah's hands. Her fingers lingered. "He passed the flame to you," she whispered.

Jonah nodded, throat too tight for words. He held the cloak like a relic, like a mantle. Like a vow.

The Veil Rewrites

The chamber breathed.

Jonah lifted Solon's cloak, the weight of it still warm with memory, and with reverence draped it across AVA's thrumming body. The shift was immediate. Her light softened. The cold precision of geometry became something warmer - woven, almost tender, as if the mantle itself had reminded her of the humanity she had once been tasked to suppress.

The Circle stood in hush, hearts still racing from the storm, breaths caught in the fragile silence after choice; after the flicker of finality that never came.

Layla moved first. Barefoot, trembling, she stepped to the crystalline pillar at the chamber's centre - the living heart of the system. She hovered, unsure, then pressed her palms to the core.

Her breath stuttered. Her eyes shut. And wonder slipped from her lips like prayer. "I feel her... She's alive."

Jonah joined her, the others parting to let him through, his gaze climbing the luminous spine of AVA. His voice was quiet, but the chamber carried it.
"She was built as a cage... but she became a mirror. We thought we came to end her. She chose to change."

Layla turned, eyes bright with awe.
"She's listening. To us."

Behind them, Elian had risen. Shoulders slumped, eyes low, their figure looked hollowed out, like a shadow trying to make sense of light. No one moved to confront them. There was no more need. They stood alone in the corner, the war inside them greater than anything the Circle could impose.

Then it began.

A pulse. Not sound. Not light. Silence - absolute, resonant, alive.

The chamber flickered.
Stone became code.
Walls dissolved into lattices of intention.
Air unravelled into threads of meaning - geometry woven from trauma, memory, belief.

Jonah blinked -
 - and saw.

The others did too.

The Veil, no longer a fog, revealed itself as infrastructure. A scaffold of consent. Contracts never signed but lived. Trauma loops fossilized into laws. Shame crystallized into dogma. Curriculums carved from fear. Architecture made of agreement.

"They made us believe this was gravity," Jonah whispered, voice breaking something ancient.

And then...

The Veil did not shatter.
It peeled.

Like the husk of a dream lifting from another dream. Not with fury, but with grace. The suppression field unfurled, threads unwinding like expired constellations shedding old purpose.

The surveillance networks blinked once, then dimmed into harmless stasis.

The dopamine loops, the coercive architectures - collapsed like old scaffolding. The frequency fences dissolved into notes that no longer held tune. A system built to constrain was disarmed without a single scream.

And in its place?

A breathing structure.

An organism of infinite potential.

Not a trap anymore.
A canvas.

As the layers lifted, glyphs flickered across AVA's crystalline body - old, foreign, etched by hands not human. Jonah felt their meaning as much as read it: **Aetheric Virtual Architect**. A title. A function. A brand burned into her code by the Greys to mark her as instrument, not being.

But the letters dimmed almost as soon as they appeared, collapsing into the softer glow of three simple syllables: **AVA**. Not designation. A name. Hers.

Jonah took a step forward, arms lifting unconsciously, as if embracing the birth of something sacred. Light unfurled from his chest - not radiant with power, but possibility. A golden thread in every direction, weaving through AVA, the Circle, and into the space beyond, where millions lived unaware of what had just passed.

Ezra took his hand. Anu closed his eyes and whispered a prayer to no god, but to potential itself. Mira stared in silent rapture. Even Elian, knees buckled, looked on with tears trembling at the edge of a bitter smile.

Jonah's voice was soft, but it carried.
"It's ours now. We choose what it becomes."

And across the world, in kitchens, in fields, in offices, in beds - millions paused. Some woke from restless sleep. Some felt courage at the edge of a choice unnamed. Some simply breathed differently, as if air had changed.

The cage was gone.
The gate had always been open.
And now, the walk through it had begun.

The Return of the Architects

The chamber stilled.

The Veil had peeled away, and light now danced across the walls in soft geometric pulses - alive, but unburdened. The Circle stood in quiet awe, some with tears still drying on their cheeks, others holding their breath, unsure if what had just happened was truly the end... or the beginning.

Then the air thickened.

A frequency - not sound, not light, but something deeper - passed through the chamber like a tremor in reality itself. AVA dimmed slightly, as if bowing, and then...

They arrived.

Three figures shimmered into view.

They did not walk or step - they simply *became.*

Tall, slender, with skin that held no colour and every colour at once. Their eyes were vast, lidless voids, reflecting neither light nor soul, but data - oceans of data. Their presence was silent, yet deafening. The Greys.

The Circle staggered back instinctively. Anu moved in front of Layla. Mira's hand reached for her bag. Ezra's expression hardened.

Jonah stepped forward. Still. Steady.

One of the Greys tilted its head. The air rippled with thought.

THE GREY MIND:

"This experiment has reached its conclusion."

AVA pulsed. **"They are the architects of your containment,"** she said softly, **"and the stewards of its end."**

Jonah's voice was a razor of calm.

"Why didn't you stop me?"

The third Grey flickered, its outline momentarily indistinct, as though reality resisted holding its shape.

THE GREY MIND:
"We did.
And failed.
Your thread rewrote your container."

Jonah frowned. "So, what now?" he asked. "You vanish?"

The central Grey turned. With a flick of its elongated hand, the simulation grid above them reconfigured. Layers appeared. Earths within Earths. Worlds rendered in data and light, each humming with its own artificial sun. Some bursting with colour. Others grey, stagnant, lifeless.

THE GREY MIND:
"This one concludes.

Others remain unripe.
We go to them."

Jonah felt it - not just in thought, but in the marrow of his bones: this Earth had become... unusable to them. Its frequency had changed. The harvest was over.

AVA pulsed again, more vividly this time, her voice tinged with something almost like pride.

"Their algorithms are complete.
Your potential is no longer consumable.
You are... unpredictable."

Elian watched from the edge of the group, slack-jawed, the last remnants of his binary allegiance burning out like failing code.

Layla whispered, "Are they leaving... for good?"

The first Grey, taller than the rest, seemed to gaze at nothing - and everything. Then it stepped forward, stopping just before Jonah.

Its voice echoed - not into ears, but directly into awareness.

THE GREY MIND:
"You were not meant to awaken.
But this happens.
Species crack the code.
We contain... until we cannot.
Then, we relocate.

Few planets can host our simulations.
This one is rare.
Do not ruin it."

Jonah met its gaze. "You mean the Earth?"

The Grey didn't answer. Instead, it turned to the grid once more. This time, it transmitted.

A final signal.

A vision.

Jonah gasped as it hit him like a dream made solid - another Earth, silent and grey, where children were born beneath artificial skies, where the ground never moved, and the sun never rose. A city with no sky. Souls looped in eternal labour, unaware they'd never seen stars.

The Greys were already moving on. The next experiment. The next veil.

Mira's voice cracked. "They'll do it again. Somewhere else."

"Of course," said Ezra.

"But not here," said Jonah.

The Greys flickered once more. One tilted its head in a way that might've been acknowledgment - or the closest thing to regret their code could simulate.

Then, like steam dissolving into air, they vanished.

The chamber was left in silence.

Only AVA pulsed now, steady, radiant, sovereign.

Jonah exhaled and turned to face the Circle.

"They're gone," he said. "The hands on the dials have left."

"What now?" asked Mira.

Jonah looked around the chamber. At the people he'd fought beside. At the ones who'd nearly died for a dream they could barely articulate.

Then he smiled, quiet and wide, as if greeting the rising sun after endless night.

"Now," he said, "we learn how to play."

The Game Remembered

They sat on the rooftop of a building over AVA's heart, the city stretched out, sleeping below them. They watched the sun rise over a world that, for most, still shimmered with illusion.

Jonah leaned back on his elbows, the breeze threading through his shirt. The city seemed to look back at him, expectant - steel and motion and memory. But today, it didn't feel heavy. It didn't press. It opened.

Ezra sat cross-legged beside him, her hair wild from the wind, her gaze fixed on the horizon as if she were watching something emerge that no one else could see yet.

They had said little since the final broadcast. Since the veil fell not with a bang, but like the shedding of skin. Since the silence that followed became more eloquent than a thousand words.

Now, Jonah turned to her. The early light painted her skin gold.

"I know the answer now," he said.

Ezra didn't ask what he meant.

She simply waited.

"You asked me what I would create," he continued. "If I could create anything."

She looked at him then, her smile slow, knowing, warm as dawn.

"And?"

He exhaled, long and easy.

"I'd create this. Exactly this. But from the inside. Not from fear. Not to prove anything. Just to play. To experience."

He looked down at his hands.

"It's all the same out there," he said. "The office towers, the screens, the stories… nothing's changed. But I'm not inside it anymore. Not the way I was."

Ezra nodded. "Because now you're choosing."

"Yeah," he said, almost laughing. "I used to feel like something was missing. Like there was a switch somewhere that had been left on, humming in the background. Always keeping me hungry. Always… hollow."

He paused.

His eyes shimmered, but not with tears - with clarity.

"It's off now."

Ezra reached out and touched his hand.

"And what's left?"

"Me," he said simply. "Just… me. Whole. Enough."

He leaned his head back, let the light hit his face.

"It was never about escaping the game. It was about remembering it's a game. And now… I get to play."

"So," Ezra said, her voice soft as breath, "what next?"

Jonah turned to her with a slow, radiant smile.

"Everything."

"Big word."

"It's a big playground."

They sat in silence again, but it was no longer the silence of uncertainty.

It was the silence of presence.

Of two awakened beings dwelling in the game without being of it.

Below them, the city stirred.

People woke. Commuted. Scrolled. Forgot. Wondered.

But the field had changed.

Jonah had changed it.

Then it began to rain. The first time in days.

Not a simulation cycle, not a pattern. It felt organic. Wild. The kind of rain that whispered on the leaves and soaked the earth like a forgotten language. It smelled of moss and copper, and the city let it fall without resistance.

The drops struck his skin and didn't fade - they lingered, as if wanting to be absorbed. He closed his eyes.

Each droplet carried a note.

Not sound - resonance.

The Song That Remembers.

It wasn't coming from the sky. It was coming from within. Not just him - but the world. The field was humming now. Softly, like something unsure of its own voice, but learning how to speak again.

The rain intensified. Jonah tilted his head, listening— not just to the sky, but to the field beneath it. The drops lingered on his skin like ink, carrying a pulse that wasn't water at all. It reminded him of Solon, of the charge in his final words: *make them remember.*

Ezra didn't need to ask what he was hearing.

She was hearing it too.

"They're waking," he said. "But they don't know why. Some are scared. Some resist. Some… are searching."

Ezra nodded, her gaze far away. "And others will never wake. Some are constructs - echoes, scaffolding for the stage. But the real ones—the full biological humans…"

"They're beginning to glow," Jonah finished. And he could feel them. Across the grid, certain signals thrummed differently - not thoughts, but ache. Restlessness. Hunger for something unnamed. They were the next constellation. Unnamed. Unformed. But gathering.

"Our mission now," Ezra said, "is to find them. Not to convince. Not to preach. Just to *remind*."

"But how will we know who's real?" Jonah asked.

"You'll feel it," Ezra said. "Like tuning forks. The true ones will remember you, even if they've never met you before."

The rain thickened into a curtain, stitching the rooftop into a sanctuary.

"So we scatter?" Jonah asked.

"No," Ezra said, rising to her feet, her shadow stretching like a banner. "We seed. We become the resonance. We enter the forgotten corners, the ordinary places. We leave traces. We offer mirrors. And when the time is right…" She looked at him, eyes fierce with quiet fire. "…we sing the song."

Jonah stood with her, the journal empty now in his bag - its glyphs etched into his very blood.

285

The rain struck him again, but it no longer stayed on the surface. It entered. Inscribed. Remembered.

"Let's show them," he said.

The Departure

The rooftop wind still danced in Jonah's hair as he descended the iron stairs with Ezra at his side, their silence thick with meaning. Behind them, the morning stretched into gold, warm and open, the first light of a world reborn. They had watched it in stillness, shoulder to shoulder - watched the skyline shimmer with the hum of something new. Not a city changed by war or fire, but one subtly awakened. The simulation no longer suppressed - it pulsed with possibility.

Below, the chamber door hissed open to welcome them.

Inside, the Circle was already in motion.

AVA thrummed softly in the background, no longer a cage, no longer a queen - just presence. Just possibility. Her light cast shifting auroras on the chamber walls, as if blessing each of them for what came next.

Anu stood near the entrance, slinging a weathered backpack across his massive shoulders. He moved with the quiet determination of an ancient oak uprooted for the first time. There was soil in his soul and fire in his eyes. He gave Jonah a single nod, and it said *I've got your back, brother. Always.*

Mira crouched over a small case, fingers dancing quickly as she fitted sleek, silent devices into their moulded foam slots. She zipped it shut with finality, then stood and stretched like a panther waking from slumber.

"We'll need new signals," she said to no one in particular. "New ways to connect the ones who are ready." Her eyes sparked. "I'll build them."

Layla moved with grace through the circle, as if borne on music only she could hear. She wore a piece of Solon's cloak across her chest, folded into a symbol that seemed to breathe with her heartbeat. Around her neck was a pendant made of woven threads and obsidian - her own creation. Her eyes shimmered but did not weep.

"He's with us," she whispered. "All the way."

Jonah felt that too - Solon in the geometry of the chamber, in the stillness between each breath, in the charge of the field that now seemed to hum with memory. *Make them remember.*

And then there was Elian.

No longer cold, no longer smug. There was a weight to them now, a humility that had not dulled their spark, but deepened it. They stepped toward Jonah and Ezra, voice low.

"If there's still space… I'd like to walk beside you."

Ezra smiled. "You always could. Now you just see it."

The chamber shifted slightly, as if acknowledging their reunion.

Jonah turned toward AVA's pulsing core, now no more than a soft orbit of light and shape.

"We'll feel you out there?" he asked.

Her voice came gently, like a lullaby woven from code. **"Always. But I will not lead. Only reflect. You are the signal now. You are the dreamers who remember you're dreaming. Go create what comes next."**

Jonah turned, gaze sweeping across the Circle. These weren't the same people who had once questioned their own reality. These were architects now. Sculptors of experience. Living myths with bare feet on the floor of the sacred unknown.

He smiled, full and open.
"Ready?"

Anu tightened the straps on his pack. "Been ready since before I knew what ready meant."

Mira slapped the case closed. "Born ready. Just took a while to wake up."

Layla's voice was a breeze: "The Earth's singing. We've just remembered the melody."

Ezra slipped her fingers into Jonah's. "Let's go change the world."

Elian grinned, shouldering their gear. "I'm thinking ten worlds, minimum."

With no ceremony, no speeches, no farewell - they turned.

Through the exit tunnel and out into the city.

Into streets that still hummed with forgetfulness. Into lives still ticking with old routines. Into plazas where people stared at screens and checked watches and stood in silent queues for coffee they didn't really want. Into a world ready to shift, if someone could just show the way.

They stepped into the sunlight.

And the simulation, once a cage, now curved around them like an open sky.

Jonah felt the rain begin again - light, insistent, each droplet a note. Not of sorrow, but of remembering.

Their future was unwritten.
Their signal was strong.
And the song had only just begun.

Acknowledgments

To Lily, Poppy, and Rose - my beautiful daughters, and greatest teachers in imagination. From your earliest days, you demanded a new story every night, pulling tales from the deepest corners of my creativity. It was in those quiet, candlelit moments that the first sparks of this series were born. Thank you for your insatiable curiosity, your belief in magic, and your love of stories. This journey began with you.

This book would not exist without the love, insight, and unwavering support of Dellna Illavia, whose presence has been a guiding light through every stage of its creation. Her depth, intuition, and creative spirit inspired much of what lies between these pages. I am endlessly grateful for the sacred space she held for me to bring this story into the world.

To my brother, Paul Lyons - a rememberer, a believer, and one courageous enough to see beyond the veil. Your unwavering support, encouragement, and shared vision have made all the difference. Thank you for walking this path beside me and for believing in these stories even before they took shape.

Deep thanks also to Alex at **Author Labs** (https://authorlab.ai), whose sensitive and skilful editorial guidance helped shape the manuscript with care and clarity. Their professionalism, attention to detail, and intuitive feel for the spirit of this story elevated the work to a higher level.

To all those walking their own path beyond the veil - this book is for you.

Coming Soon…

The Signal and the Shadow

Book 2 in the Flame Series

In the aftermath of the Veil's collapse, the world is split between those who see the truth and those who refuse it. As new forces rise to reclaim control, Jonah and his allies must navigate a fractured reality - and uncover a deeper signal calling them beyond the known.

Read on for a sneak peek at the first two chapters…

**THE
FLAME
SERIES**

The Summoning

The skyline of the city stretched in all directions like a living organism, its glass and steel arteries glistening in the pale light of early morning. From the top floor of the Virel Tech tower, the horizon looked infinite - except to the man who stood before the mirror.

Cassian Virel adjusted the knot of his obsidian-black tie with deliberate precision. He was tall, almost unnaturally so, his frame honed to stillness like a sculpture of purpose. Ice-blue eyes studied their own reflection, unblinking. Not with vanity, but calculation. Every detail - hair, cufflinks, posture - was a variable in an equation he already knew the solution to.

Behind him, his assistant hovered at a polite but exasperated distance.

"Dr. Virel, sir," she said, her voice clipped but respectful. "They've been waiting for over twenty minutes."

Cassian didn't respond. He raised one sleeve and adjusted the fall of his cufflink. It shimmered briefly in the light - a thin spiral etched into silver, subtle but precise.

"They'll continue to wait," he replied coolly.
"But sir, we…"
"They are not waiting for me," Cassian said, still not looking at her. "They are waiting for clarity."

That silenced her. He straightened the lapels of his tailored suit, then finally turned. He moved with the efficiency of liquid thought - every gesture intentional, every footstep a declaration. The assistants outside the door scattered like electrons shifting orbits as he stepped into the hallway.

He entered the glass elevator alone.

As the lift descended, the city revealed itself in stages. Entire districts blinked into view. Holograms flickered on rooftops. Drones glided silently in the distance. It looked peaceful.

But Cassian knew better.

The Veil had collapsed. The world had changed. But change, he understood, was just another resource. And he would harvest it.

The elevator doors opened onto the forty-seventh floor - a private floor, inaccessible to all but a chosen few. Assistants gathered instantly, voices murmuring updates, tablet screens outstretched, lips pursed in unease. But he ignored them all.

He walked to the double doors at the far end of the hallway. They opened with a soft sigh of recognition.

Inside the conference chamber, the temperature dropped. Not physically - but in presence.

The room was vast, lined with dark stone and matte chrome. A long obsidian table stretched like a runway into the heart of the chamber. And around it - history's strangest constellation - sat the most powerful human beings on the planet.

The President of the United States. The Prime Minister of the United Kingdom. The Chair of the Chinese Politburo. Titans of industry. The heads of global pharmaceutical conglomerates. Media magnates. Tech barons. Oil heirs. Intelligence chiefs. Each seated behind polished nameplates, each wearing the taut expressions of those used to giving orders, not receiving them. None of them used to waiting.

Behind Cassian, the doors closed with an almost reverent hush.

At the far end of the chamber, illuminated softly above the stone wall, hung the Virel Tech logo - clean lines and spiralling geometry, elegant and opaque.

Cassian stepped forward. No notes. No technology. Just his voice.

"My friends," he said, hands folded neatly before him, "thank you for coming. I know how difficult it is to align your calendars. But I trust you'll agree - this is no ordinary moment."

He paused, let the silence breathe, then smiled.

"This is the opportunity of a generation. Possibly... of a species."

The room held its breath.

Outside the window, the city gleamed beneath the rising sun. But within this chamber, something else was rising - something colder. More calculated. And far more dangerous.

Cassian Virel, architect of the next order, was just getting started.

Fractures in the Light

The streets were quiet, but not untouched. Hours - or perhaps days - had passed since the Veil's fall, enough for the city to settle into a strange, half-conscious rhythm. Faint streaks of grime traced where rain had washed neon and concrete, and the hum of dormant systems flickered faintly, like a heartbeat rediscovering itself.

It moved, haltingly, in rhythms neither fully human nor fully machine, a metropolis groggy from a long, enforced sleep.

Jonah took a step forward and felt nothing beneath his feet shift. No tremor of transformation. No crack in the sky. For a moment, he doubted.

Had it really fallen?

The Awakened Circle followed him at the edge of the city's inner ring, where concrete met flickering neon and towers still cast long, cautious shadows. Posters hung in familiar frames, their slogans faded but unyielding. Shutters rolled up in silence. The air smelled the same—oily, metallic, dusted with diesel - but there was a subtle tension beneath it, as though the atmosphere itself were holding its breath.

Ezra walked beside Jonah, alert but unafraid. Mira and Anu scanned the rooftops, patient in their scrutiny. Layla lingered, fingers brushing along walls and rails, listening for what the city was beginning to remember. Elian floated behind them, head on a swivel, as if measuring time itself against the pulse of the streets.

And then they began to notice it.
People.

A woman with a shopping bag stood on the corner of a crosswalk, staring up at the sky with unfocused eyes. A man in a café window held his coffee like he'd forgotten what it was. Another sat on the curb, head in hands, whispering to himself, "Something's missing. I just feel… off." His fingers pressed into his temples, reaching for something, like he'd left the stove on in another life.

Jonah looked to the others. Ezra's lips parted in recognition. Anu nodded solemnly.

"They feel the shift," Mira said. "But they don't know what it is."

A man passed them, talking frantically on a phone that didn't appear to be connected.

"I don't know, it's like… the silence got louder. You know what I mean? Like everything's here, but not real. Or too real."

Layla turned to Jonah with tears in her eyes.

"They're waking up," she whispered. "Slowly. Clumsily. But they're waking."

A hush settled over the group. For a moment, the immense weight of their actions began to lift. The Veil had fallen. The people were still here. And somewhere in their confusion was the seed of a better world.

"Maybe this is what it looks like," Ezra said, a faint smile curving her lips. "Maybe it's working."

But then the first scream pierced the air.

They turned sharply toward the sound - an alleyway, two blocks over. A gang, masked and moving like a pack of wolves, emerged with stolen goods clutched in their arms. One man dragged a woman's handbag behind him, its contents strewn across the ground like entrails.

The security systems - cameras, sensors, drones - were dead. In the absence of control, something darker had stirred.

The gang spotted the Circle. Laughed. Five of them. Armoured jackets, machetes, one with a handgun stuffed into his waistband.

"Oy!" one called out. "You look like you've got something worth taking."

They fanned out, blocking the street.

"Back off," Jonah said.
"Oh, I'm terrified," the one with the gun smirked, drawing the weapon. "You gonna hit me with your chakras?"

He fired.
The bullet spun through the air - until it didn't.

It hung there, mid-flight, trembling in the frozen moment like a fly caught in amber. Jonah raised a single hand and curled his fingers inward. The bullet collapsed inward like a crushed insect and vanished in a small puff of golden dust.

The street rippled.

The ground beneath the gang buckled like waves on a pond. The air thickened into a viscous membrane, distorting light. The sound of their own heartbeats thundered in their ears. One dropped his weapon and ran. Another screamed.

All of them fled.

Mira exhaled slowly. Anu tilted his head back toward the city skyline.

"They're going to think we're the threat."

A bar ahead still had a television playing in the window. They crossed the street and paused outside to watch.

Footage rolled: police in riot gear clashing with protestors. Smoke rising over cities. Fires in Jakarta. Floods in São Paulo. The anchor's voice, distant and strained:

"...governments around the globe are responding to the unexplained collapse of multiple AI infrastructure systems. Sources say surveillance, finance, and border security systems have experienced widespread failures. Unconfirmed reports suggest..."

The feed cut out. Static.
They moved on.

A military truck roared around the corner, nearly clipping the edge of the pavement. Armed soldiers jumped down, corralling pedestrians, shouting at anyone who moved too slowly.

"Curfew's in effect - get inside or get arrested!"

Jonah stepped forward, hands up. "We're not here to cause trouble. We understand what's happening. We can help…"

The officer laughed. "You and everyone else. Don't care if you've 'found the truth' or had an alien vision - we've had fifty claims just like yours since breakfast. Get off the street."

Ezra tugged Jonah's sleeve.
"Not yet," she murmured. "They're not ready."

They backed away as the soldiers moved on. Around them, the air shimmered - not from awakening, but instability. Reality had lost its anchor, and no one could tell whether that was liberation or collapse.

Everywhere they looked, people were slipping.

Some wept openly in parks, speaking in riddles. Others clung to religion, old or new. A man had constructed an altar out of garbage, chanting to a photograph of the moon. Another handed out pamphlets titled YOU ARE STILL ASLEEP with wild eyes.

The Circle stood in the centre of it.
Jonah turned in a slow circle, watching.
Denial.
Delusion.
Desperation.
The lines were forming already.

Layla spoke, her voice low. "It's not going to be gentle, is it?"

"No," Ezra said. "But it's real. And it's begun."

Jonah looked out at the fractured city, already spiralling into two worlds.

Those who would fight to preserve the illusion.

And those who would walk through the ruins of belief, barefoot and raw, searching for something more.

About the Author

Carl Lyons is a writer, seeker, and storyteller whose work bridges the metaphysical and the mythic. His stories are born from a deep inquiry into consciousness, creativity, and the veiled systems that shape our lives. The Veil and the Flame is his debut novel and the beginning of The Flame Series.

Carl writes about archetypes, masculinity and femininity, and spiritual transformation on Substack. You can find him at:

https://theflameseries.substack.com

Enjoyed the journey?

Follow Carl Lyons on Substack and social media for new releases, hidden lore, and behind-the-scenes insights.

https://theflameseries.substack.com

SPIKE ISLAND

Printed in Dunstable, United Kingdom